STATE OF NATURE

a Charlemagne File

K.A. Bachus

Charlemagne File Timelines

Short Stories
A Lighter Shade of Night,
mid 60s to early 70s

Novels
Trinity Icon, early 70s
Cetus Wedge, early 80s
Brevet Wedge, nine months later
Lion Tamer, five months later
State of Nature, early 90s
Vory, a year later
Swallow, five weeks later
Quiet Move, late 90s
Goat Rope, 1999

CONTENTS

ONE

He belched before he spoke. He introduced every new paragraph with a frog call from deep within his ponderous belly. Mara did not mind it. She was used to better manners in worse men, but this one's habits did not bother her. He was good company and competent guidance and that was all that mattered in the field.

She turned at every belch because it sounded like a throat clearing, a summons to attend. Her manners were impeccable and ingrained and nearly cost her the operation. If she had not turned back quickly, she would have missed what she was looking for, what they had spent six weeks holed up in a deserted room over a derelict store to look for.

"You know, Mara," said Seal through a mouthful of redolent pastrami (with mustard and sauerkraut, my girl, don't forget), "I wonder about you sometimes. I like looking at you, but I like wondering, too."

Mara concentrated on her job, peering past the greasy smear Seal had left on the binocular lens during his watch, and past the decade of dirt on the window before her. She watched the news vendor at the corner below make change for a customer. "Yes," she said aloud, to show that she was listening.

"I mean, take the name for instance." Seal took a long pull on a straw in a can of cola, fully leaded—none of that diet shit for me, girl. He followed it with a particularly satisfying belch.

Mara stopped herself from turning and concentrated again on the vendor. Her arms were tired. She did not encourage Seal to continue.

Seal swept the thin, graying hair back from his forehead with podgy fingers, leaving a suggestion of mustard on his right temple.

"That name of yours is famous, girl. Did you know that?"

Mara's rudeness in not answering did not affect him. He continued.

"Yup. Sobieski's a famous name in the biz. Not strictly our business, you understand, but a branch of it. No, not CI and I still don't know why you're in this lousy division. Somebody told me you volunteered, but that's absurd. You'd have to be nuts, and you ain't nuts. Must've been an enemy of yours who told me that, girl. You got any enemies, honey?"

Mara did not move.

"Whew, you're a cold one, anyway. Never wrong and never warm, and that reminds me." Seal shifted on the old sofa that was the only furniture in the room. He crumpled the bag his pastrami had come in and threw it onto a growing pile in the corner.

"What was I saying? Oh, yeah. Sobieski. He was a legend when I came to the biz. 'Course, I got tapped for Counter Intelligence right away, but one of my buddies from training went upstairs and sometimes I saw him in the cafeteria. That was a long time ago, and he'd tell me stories about all the great killers there is in the world. I liked hearing his stories 'cause all I'd ever done at that time was run background checks on Ma 'n Pa Apple Pie and their kin. This Sobieski guy was a mean one, though, what they called an ace, a solo specialist. Those are terms you should learn, girl, especially as your name's Sobieski. So your grand-daddy Sobieski, oh, I know he ain't no relation, but he'd have to be your granddaddy if he was because he was dead before you were even thought of. Now there's a thought."

Seal's voice trailed off. He must be falling asleep. *Rejoice.* Mara held her binoculars with one arm, let the other drop, and stretched to give it a rest.

But he resumed. "He had a boy, you know. I know that because my buddy felt sorry for me, cooped up in CI all those years, and so he took me to a place called a sovereign house. Know what that is?" Seal did not wait for an answer. "It's a place where people can meet without shooting each other. Hard to ex-plain, but there are rules in the black world and my friend by that time knew his way around pretty good. He took me to one of these here places—it was in

New York City—and he said to me 'Seal, we've hit pay dirt. They're here.'

"I didn't know what the hell he was talking about, but I followed his eyes to a table over on the west side of the room, and let me tell you, girl, in those places, it's important which side of the room you sit on. You may need to know that someday, and I've just told you. Somebody'll probably train you in that event, but if they forget, you just remember old Seal told you it's fucking important. You can have all the rules you want about shooting people over a drink, but they ain't worth nothing if you put deadly enemies at the same table with guns and intentions."

There was no sign of a letup in Seal's monologue. Mara rested the other arm.

"Anyhow, at this here table on the west side of the place were these three guys. They were at their best in those days; ain't heard much about 'em since, but then I ain't been in a position to hear much about nothing. The tallest one had black hair; they called him the Frenchman. The shortest one, now this is where your famous name comes in, honey, he had those deep-set Slavic eyes, and my friend says to me 'That's Sobieski.' Well, I give him a surprised look and he explains. 'Son of,' he says. The third guy was the one that made me shudder, though. He was like a blond piece of sculpture, perfect and still, and my friend tells me they call him Mack in the biz, so to speak, because he cuts throats for a living, silent and sure, and he's sort of in charge of the team, for that's what they were—still are, for all I know, though I doubt they're still alive, but they could be for sure. The name was Charlemagne, the team name, that is. That's a name that was only whispered back then. They were the best, got the best prices, because they never, ever failed."

Mara picked up a radio from the windowsill with her rested arm.

"That's him," she said into it, "headed east on Fourth."

"We got him?" Seal heaved himself from the sofa and took the binoculars from her. He did not see her nod as he watched his street crew round up vendor and customer, quietly, as in a pantomime. "How do you know?"

"He is the only one whose paper was handed to him. Every day. All the other customers picked up their own."

Mara's voice matched her hair, blonde and smooth like a slow river flowing over round stones. Seal loved to look at her and listen to her and he took in his fill now, regretting the end of the operation. He was sure she would be moved up. Had to be. She sure didn't belong in CI.

"I was telling you about Charlemagne," he said, noting the change in her eyes, a change that would be imperceptible to a less experienced man. "I was telling you because it's funny. You've got a name like Sobieski and it's a big name in the biz, in the biz of the upstairs folks, that is, and I'm sure you're destined for better things, honey. But if I had to say who you bring to mind, it ain't Sobieski, though I suppose there's a touch of the Slav about those green eyes of yours. Nope. The guy you bring to my mind is Mack. You're like him—toxic and exquisite, and I'm gonna miss ya."

"I'm not going anywhere, Seal."

He sighed. "I just hope I taught you a few things to take with you."

"We're a team, old man." Mara put the binoculars in their case and slung the strap over her shoulder. Her ponytail gleamed in the fading afternoon light as she opened the stairwell door opposite the window. "Hurry up or we'll lose gloating privileges."

Seal sighed again before following his pupil to the interrogation.

TWO

The afternoon desert heat kept the laundry room empty. Hot water washes and tumble drying only improved the place.

The heat insured privacy. In cooler parts of the day, Mara could walk more comfortably back and forth to wash her clothes, past the apartment complex pool, past the picnic area, into the laundry, and back again to her apartment, but that required hellos and smiles and polite answers to rude inquiries. How these Californians liked to pry!

Mara wore shorts and sandals and a loose blue t-shirt with the inscription 'It's a CInch' that only Seal and her classmates in training would understand. More training than Seal ever imagined alerted her now, well before the event happened. She armed herself with a cup of bleach.

"Hi." He smiled beautifully, a shining, merry smile, like Louis's, but without the underlying malice.

"Hi." Mara kept her grip on the measuring cup.

"I am Sergei Pavlenko."

"Yes, I know." She waited and studied him for the clues that were not present in photos she had seen. His straight, light brown hair was unruly, or else ruffled by the stiff, hot desert wind. No, that was surely a cowlick in back. She remembered her father's struggle against a mop just like it and smiled.

Sergei Pavlenko smiled back.

"What do you want?" Mara recovered the mistake, barking the question and holding the bleach further in front of her.

He stepped forward. She raised her arm and he stopped.

"I need your help."

The washing machine behind her began a noisy spin cycle. This was not a subject to be shouted, but she did not want him to come any closer. She raised her voice, hoping no one else would hear her.

"No deals, Pavlenko, I got them; iron tight. If they were yours, I'm sorry, but that's the game."

He raised a Slavic eyebrow and smiled again. "They were not mine, but congratulations anyway. You have a knack." He looked around the room. "Is there someplace we can go—to talk? You can get your weapon if you do not trust me. I understand. I will wait for you here. See, you have plenty of room to leave safely. Get your weapon and come back for me. I won't follow you to your apartment. I will wait here. Go. Go."

He set a plastic chair against the far gallery of dryers and sat down on it, well away from the entrance. Sweat beaded on his forehead, but he did not move to wipe it away.

Mara did as he suggested and was well armed with her Glock and a plan for a rendezvous when she returned for her laundry.

...

She had picked someplace trendy, but not too crowded. The decor, old-world California-style, provided some privacy, with deep booths and staggered floor levels. The plastic stained glass poured colored lights over oak tables pretending to be antiques.

For the benefit of their waitress, Mara and Sergei feigned a casual conversation while she kept her Glock pointed at him through the handbag in her lap and he kept his hands above the table. They sat in the smoking section, because, he said, he smoked, and indeed he did. A careful upbringing and many hours of Seal's company had prepared her for nuisances. She waved away the smoke.

"I see you are right-handed," he told her in Russian. "Unlike your father."

Mara replied in the same language while the waitress lingered in the area, filling coffee mugs in front of them, then water glasses, though they had not asked for water.

"What do you know of my father? He is long dead—of no concern to you."

Pavlenko did not answer immediately. The waitress hovered, expecting an order. He shook his head, and she found some other errand in the kitchen. He continued in Russian.

"I know much. About him; about his, um, associates. I was trained by the man who arranged your father's death."

"I did not see you there that day." Mara did not hide her contempt.

The waitress came back like a pesky fly. Mara forced herself to lighten her grip on the trigger.

Sergei put out his cigarette, blowing the last of it over her head as he leaned back in his seat. He waved away the pesky fly and the waitress left, pretending to have something else to do.

"Your father was my special study," he said. "I wrote my training thesis on him. It was very good. I was destined for a brilliant career." He grinned at her. "Then the wall came down."

"A great tragedy."

"A shocking bore. During the Cold War, you knew what side you were on. Your friends and enemies were distinct. Now they are muddled. Everybody's thinking is muddled. Mine is itself a dark cloud."

"You have my sympathy." There was, of course, no sympathy in her voice.

He stared into Mara's steady green eyes. Her arm did not move, but he had no doubt it would take her no more than a twitch to pull the trigger under the table. "Your whole supply of sympathy?" he asked.

"Every molecule."

"Then I am rich indeed." He looked away, looked down, then up, mastering the rancid taste of business that rose in his throat as he spoke to this exquisite young woman.

"I am sorry about your father," he said, trying to look as though he meant it.

Mara was not buying it. She said nothing.

Back again, the waitress would not go away this time, so they perused their menus. Mara held hers with one hand. Sergei began a monologue in fast, quiet Russian as his eyes scanned the lunch list.

"I need your help. I promised myself I would not begin with that. Let me try again. I am having some difficulty staying alive. I cannot tell you why because I do not trust you, though I come to you as the only hope of trust that I can have. I once was sworn to kill your father and his associates and now that the world has turned inside out, they are the only ones I know. That is, I know them. I studied them and did my best to defeat them. But all I once knew is dissolving. Somehow, I cannot conceive of Charlemagne dissolving, can you?"

"You did your best."

"I said I was sorry."

"That brings him back to life then. He was not armed that day."

"He was not?" Doubt. He chewed his lower lip. "He did not abandon his beliefs? He did not embrace some other philosophy, did he?"

"No." Mara paused. Pavlenko deserved nothing, no explanation, but she noticed a hunted look, man as quarry, and recognized it. "My father liked to escape the game sometimes," she explained. "He pretended he lived a different life."

"Yes. Yes. He would. It explains his women. They were as removed from the game as possible, every time. I was young and did not understand the dossier then. Yes. That explains it." Sergei looked up sharply. "Until he married your mother, of course."

The waitress cleared her throat. They ordered to make the woman happy and headed off her first personal question by pretending not to understand it.

"Why are Americans so prying?" he asked when she had gone. "You have studied them. Tell me."

"I am an American."

"You know what I mean. You are as much an outsider as I am. But you know more. I can get your Polish citizenship back for you, you know. Your father never gave it up. Or I could do that a week ago. Now, I don't know. Tell me why Americans pry."

"It is an open society," she said. "Privacy is unknown; secrecy not trusted. People discuss the most intimate aspects of their lives in everyday conversations."

"Shocking."

"No. Just tawdry. But it is impolite to show boredom. One must be interested."

"A legacy of capitalism, no doubt."

The waitress set his soup before him, saving Mara a useless conversation.

"Are you going to eat that salad?" he said. "May I relieve you of it?" He reached across and dragged the plate toward him without waiting for her answer. "Why did you order Italian dressing? I like French. No, no, I insist on helping you in this way. You can keep your finger on the trigger, do you see, inconspicuously. I like chicken, too. I am glad you ordered it."

Mara watched him eat. His nails were grimy, arms dirty. She noticed odd patches he had missed in shaving. A long scrape ran under his shirt from his left ear. He fought to keep his eyes open.

Mara smiled.

The smile arrested him, mid-chew. Mara was no longer a mere beauty. She became cute, adorable, surely incapable of firing the loaded weapon in her bag. There was no charm like this in his world, in their world. Where did she get it? He soaked himself in it, knowing better. But hope is hope.

His thoughts were transparent to Mara. How many times had her father and the others come home —shot to pieces it seemed, filthy, tired, disgusted— and looked at her that way? She was no threat; there-fore, he was no threat. When the chicken came, she let go of the trigger and picked up the fork with her right hand.

"How long do you have?" she asked him.

"To eat?" he asked. "Or to live?"

THREE

Michael played Chopin. Mara hated to interrupt him, but she must finish the interview, and if successful, fly back to the States within the day. Seal did not know she was gone.

She crossed the parquet floor of the small ball-room, walking toward Michael's back.

"Mara! What are you doing at home?" He spoke German and did not turn around, finishing the Nocturne before standing to meet her. He held her by the shoulders, kissed her cheek, said all the platitudes, and waited, smiling.

"You are as incredible as your father," she said, "with eyes in the back of your head. I was very quiet."

"You were, but not quiet enough. And he is our father, ...Sister." He did not let go of her shoulders.

"When—how—did you find out?"

"Yesterday. Your mother told me—us. Papa is in a state. Your timing is awkward."

"It has never been anything else, but I must see him. Now. Was it a surprise to you?"

He shook his head. "Not for me. I have suspected for years now." He led her to the mirrored south wall, where the parquet floor seemed to repeat itself forever. They stood side by side.

"Look at us," Michael said.

They were separated by fifteen centimeters, ten years, and gender. Was her blonde hair a trifle darker? Her eyes were green, not blue, but light eyes are light eyes seen two meters from a mirror. They had the same training. His had been more intense, and more practiced. He was a musical genius, she reflected, while she was merely competent, without talent in that area. She marveled at the lottery that is inheritance.

"Papa, on the other hand, was stunned," he said. "Which is amazing. He observes so much and never saw this. Look. We are so obvious. Even with different mothers. You look more like me than Nadia did." He turned toward the staircase on their left. "I will take you upstairs and announce you before I go riding."

She followed him across the polished floor, making no sound. There was an echo, though, when she said, "You will need to be there. This is operational."

Michael laughed and the echo laughed, too. "He has found out that you are his natural daughter, his long-lost Nadia come back to life, God bless her sainted soul, and you think you are going to discuss operations?" He laughed again, put his arm around her shoulder, and squeezed affectionately. "You will be lucky to leave home to go shopping. Maybe next year."

"Here is Mara, Papa," Michael said as he dragged her through the vaulted door of the office. "I told her she might go shopping next year."

Misha stood behind his desk, his sleeves rolled to the elbow, leaning over a map. Behind him, the walls were covered with more maps, some political, some geographic, a few on cork boards with colored push pins, others behind lighted plexiglass marked by grease pencil. He looked up. The gray hair at the edges only dulled the otherwise brilliant blond hair at his temples. There were more lines in his face than in Michael's, and a long scar down his neck, an operational token. Mara remembered the day he had come home with that.

Misha shook his head. "I will find her a suitable husband before then."

Was Misha joking? Did Misha joke? Could she think of an instance? Everybody feared this man. She never did. Hated, resented, respected, in varying amounts at different times, but never feared. He would not cut her throat, she knew, but marry her off to some weak-chinned European aristocrat? Here was true danger. Her tightrope frayed. To be disobedient would reflect badly on the beloved Vasily. To obey meant what? A life of tepid luxury as opposed to…? Standing for hours in a squalid room with Seal? She shuddered before she could catch it and noticed him smile at it. Joking and smiling, both in one day, a red-letter day.

"I am not joking," he said.

Misha was always one to put people at ease.

"Oh dear," she replied.

"Do not think you will get around me with that smile."

"Of course not."

"I assume you have come to your senses and walked away from that silly job."

"Then you are slipping."

He took the bait but spat out the hook. "I will allow you…"

"Allow me!"

"Yes. I will allow you this one operation because you are foolishly trying to help someone else. It is not likely to last long. Your role is to be purely support-ive. You will do as I tell you, stay out of danger, and give your resignation to the Americans at the end of it."

"I agree to none of this."

"Is it that seedy boss of yours? Is he in trouble again?"

Again? Mara shook herself. "You are not listening to me, Sir. I do not agree."

"I am not interested in your agreement."

Mara heard her voice rise and strove to bring it under control. "You are my stepfather now that my mother married you," she said through clenched teeth, "but you are not and have never been my father, no matter what the genetics may be. I am an Ameri-can citizen and Vasily Sobieski's daughter. I will use my name and my talent to benefit my country."

"Is this rehearsed?" Misha sat down in a comfort-able leather chair, indicated a plain wooden one across the desk. "Sit."

Mara felt grateful for the five-foot expanse of ma-hogany between them.

"Mara, I consider a woman who kills an abomina-tion. Especially if it is for her country."

He used his patient tone, the one reserved for women, children, and idiots. Mara suspected that, to him, she fit all three. His tone was triple smooth, his best attempt at putting a person at ease. It failed, of course. It was impossible to be easy in Misha's presence.

"That is nonsense and I do not kill," she said. "I am in counterintelligence, a quiet branch of it. Very routine."

He raised his eyebrow in an eloquent Oh, yeah? An expression that he would never be so low as to say. "Who is this friend for whom you risk my displeasure and perhaps my life, if it is not Seal?"

He knows Seal. Of course, he knows Seal. Probably has a copy of his personnel file. Probably knows what Seal had for dinner yesterday. No doubt he can smell the pastrami on my clothes. *I traveled six thousand miles to give him this intelligence.* She said, "It is not a friend. It is an enemy."

Misha sat forward, his forearms on the desk before him, and waited.

"I do not know why I believe him," she said, "or even if I believe him enough to bother you with this. He is Sergei Pavlenko."

"He came to you? For what?"

"I don't think it is a trap."

"I did not say it was."

"But you thought it."

"You are improving," Misha said through an almost smile. "Tell me why it is not a trap."

"Because he was too weary to be faking his fear."

FOUR

Everything was wrong. Every single thing. Every alarm, every signal, every safeguard had been tripped. The doorknob was bloody. Mara held her gun hidden by her side and worked the key left-handed. She slipped the door open slightly, waiting, more open, more waiting. Yes, Papa, you brought up a good daughter. A daughter who knows how to use her gun, knows she will use it, knows she will regret using it. A daughter who will live or die free, not locked up safely at home, nor gunned down on a final night at the opera, like little Nadia. That's what you wanted, Papa, to be normal. Normal—more or less.

She felt the trigger rest, the round chambered, the hammer cocked. There was no sound inside her apartment. Noisy children were coming down the stairs around the corner. They could come through only one way. They would pass her door. She slipped inside her living room. No one, no sound. She pushed the door closed behind her and locked it softly, left-handed. No point in being ambushed from behind. The children passed the door, their laughter fading as they headed for the pool. Mara saw bright flashes of pink and green through the edges of the blinds as they passed the kitchen window to her left. Blots and dabs of brown, and clots of viscous red made a trail on the carpet to her bedroom.

Mara checked the hall closet on her way. She did not care to be shot in the back, or taken from behind, or... Did Misha really cut people's throats? This she had heard from other sources before Seal mentioned it. Such details were not discussed at home. Her training had included many things, very effective things, in the martial arts and the use of weapons, many weapons, but not that, though she knew the theory. Misha had a knife, sure. Presumably... How much could heredity account for anyway? Was there an appreciable difference between growing up the daughter and granddaughter of two world-famous political assassins and discovering she was the biological daughter of the deadliest?

Her bedroom was empty but rumpled. She had not left it this way. In the bathroom to her left, something choked and gurgled. She pushed with her left hand and pointed with her right. The door swung open slowly, stuck on a bloody towel. Swirled smears of blood pointed toward the far end of the little room, where the bleeder sat crumpled between the toilet and the wall.

"You are very, very good, Masha. I did not hear you or I would have fired."

"I'm glad you didn't. My neighbors hear everything. Are you finished here, Sergei Nickolaevich? Shall I help you to bed?" Mara did not put down her gun, because Sergei still covered his loosely as it lay on the floor beside him.

"Your Russian is very pretty," he said. "But that should not surprise. Your mother's father was Feodor Dolnikov, wasn't he? The older Sobieski's babysitter? I wonder what he felt when your mother married his specialist's son. Did you learn your Russian from that grandfather? Dolnikov was a respected enemy. Even enemies must find it disgraceful to be too close to the trigger." He paused to gasp. "I killed two last night. The others ran. How did you know my patronymic?"

"Take your hand off your gun, Sergei, and I will help you into bed. Stop leering that way. You are in no condition. Who did this?" She pulled his damp shirt away from the skin.

"I want to discuss philosophy. Start with death. Does one who kills begin to die?"

"We begin to die at birth, Sergei Nickolaevich. Who did this?" She probed the round wound in his belly. Fresh blood, mostly clotted, almost black.

"My friends, of course. And my enemy comes to save me. Did you see him? Mack, I mean. The Americans named him Mack, because of his knife. I am quite well acquainted with the culture, you see. I have seen Mack's mark. This is nothing compared... blood everywhere. You call him Misha. Am I correct? I read files, too. Did you get my patronymic from the Americans? Or from Mack?"

"You have no fever. Stop acting delirious."

"I am not acting. Delirious or otherwise. I am ... I need a word."

"Overwrought," she said in English.

"Good word. In pain is better. There must be an even better one in Russian. I am not emotionless like Mack. I cannot kill and then sip cognac with a bloody hand."

Did Misha do that? *Would he?* It seemed to be part of the enemy's folklore. Mara dabbed the wound with a gauze pad soaked with alcohol.

"Owww! Oh! That is terrible. Stop!"

"He hates his wounds being dressed as much as you do."

"Does he?" Sergei lifted his head off the pillow and watched her, frowning. "Does he vomit? It was not the bullet that made me use the toilet."

Mara considered. "I have seen him sick, certainly, but I did not know the reason."

"He says nothing under interrogation," said Sergei. Their eyes met briefly. "Or so I have heard. Nor did your father."

Mara cut a ten-inch length of cloth surgical tape with scissors. "And Louis?"

"The Frenchman? He screams obscenities."

Yes, of course.

"The young one sings. Songs, I mean. It is very irritating."

"So you have heard."

Sergei said nothing.

Mara helped him sit up. She bound his abdomen with an elastic bandage over the gauze.

"The American reminds me of your father sometimes. He is very fast. Your father could beat a man to death in minutes. I lost several agents just on the rumors of it."

"You have met Steve and Michael? I must have been in school. I do not remember being told of it."

Sergei did not reply immediately. "We had them once. Briefly."

They were silent for what seemed a long time. Mara took his pulse for something to do. His knuckles were calloused. New scrapes had done little damage. He was about Michael's age, say somewhere in his early thirties, well built, and in top condition for a man with a bullet in him. He had lost some blood and was continuing to lose it, though slowly, she decided. He was not turning yellow. There was time.

"Will they be there too, do you suppose?" he asked. "Yes, of course," he answered himself.

The weary, hopeless look took possession of his face again, and while she considered that he likely deserved it, Mara found herself perhaps not so far as the point of pity, but at least up to the edge of regret.

"Get some sleep now. I must make the arrangements."

"Masha?"

"Yes?"

But he was already asleep.

FIVE

S eal sat alone in his apartment at the end of a low-boy lounger sofa long decayed. He pointed a remote control at a widescreen television in the corner: channel change, volume up, volume down, channel change. He had been through forty channels a dozen times this evening. The night was young.

"Shit," he said aloud when the phone rang. He had found an episode of *Lucy* that he did not remember seeing. Was that possible? The phone rang again. Should he tape it? His finger hovered over the VCR record button. No point. He would get only half of it. The phone rang again. Anyway, should he erase the tape in the machine? Was there a tape in the machine?

He drained his beer, reached for the phone on the table next to him, picked it up because it insisted, and breathed a beery "Yeah?" into the mouthpiece.

...

He drank coffee while he shaved, spilled some on his t-shirt, changed, spilled again, said "what the fuck," half a dozen times, and left the shirt on until the coffee ran out, then changed again. He anointed himself with splashes from the fancy black bottle of men's cologne his sister sent him for Christmas. He splashed the mirror, too, and grinned at the dripping streaks as he brushed his teeth. Yeah. It had to be intelligence related. Probably something going on with the people in the upstairs division, where Mara belonged without a doubt, famous name and all. He was needed for a briefing maybe. She wanted him for a reference probably. He stuffed some less decrepit specimens of underwear and a few cleanish shirts into a carryall and danced to the door, a jerky but joyful movement that shook the remote control off the little table.

No contest, he decided. Old Lucy could never compete with the prospect of spending a few days with a girl like Mara.

He checked his back frequently. Joy and confidence grew as he crossed the parking lot and entered the labyrinth of sidewalks that led to Mara's apartment. He was Bond, James Bond. He had not felt like this since training. How long ago was that? That was way back, before dirty and gut-wrenching even, which was before tedious and mind-numbing. He knocked on her door.

Shave and a haircut, two bits.

She opened right away. She wore yellow rubber gloves and held a sponge.

"What are you doing?" he asked as he closed and locked the door behind him. He pretended for one more minute that this was not business. His nose told him it was, but he ignored it. What was that smell? Besides the disinfectant?

"I'm cleaning up the blood stains," she said. She knelt and sponged the carpet. There was a bucket of soapy water next to her. Wet spots made a trail to the hallway. "I have to pay a cleaning fee if I leave stains on the carpet."

She finished with that stain and stood up.

"So what's going on?" he asked.

She took off the gloves and checked her nails. "Come into the kitchen."

He followed her and carried the bucket for her. She turned on the radio while he poured the bloody, soapy water down the kitchen sink.

"You went to some fancy East Coast school, didn't you?" he asked her, trying to avoid the inevitable revelation, whatever it was. "Ivy league wasn't it?"

She smiled and he melted, as usual.

Mara took a cotton towel out of a drawer and dried the bucket. "I need you to get us both a few days off, Seal. I thought I could do this by myself, but there has been a glitch. Can you come with me?"

"Where?"

"I suppose you have a need to know, but first tell me if you can get us leave."

"Yes, I can."

"And will you?"

"Of course. Now tell me."

"Later. First, we need a car."

"Mine's parked outside."

"Not that one. How much is a used car? One that will get us, say, as far as Seattle?"

"Are we going to Seattle?" He wanted to shake her. He did not appreciate being handled, though he knew he would continue to do everything she said, like an insect in a web bouncing to the spider's step.

"Maybe," she answered. "How much is a car? A fast car."

"I can probably get one for seven or eight grand, but...."

She took a bag of flour from a cabinet and rummaged through it, bringing out a baggie stuffed with money. It reminded him of something. God, don't let this be a drug thing.

She counted out ten thousand dollars, in hundreds. "Make sure it has a radio," she said.

Had to be drugs.

She opened the silverware drawer, lifted the tray, and took out two plastic cards. "You probably shouldn't use your own name."

"I can go get my...."

"No. Not your official game name, either, Seal. Here. I made this for you. Be Stan Bremmer for now."

He looked at the plastic cards in his hand. One was a California driver's license. Where did she get the picture? The other was a credit card.

"The credit card is no good, though." Her voice came through his confusion. "I didn't have time to match numbers, so don't use it."

He was scared. He didn't shake or anything stupid like that. He just didn't move. Like that time back then.

"Go, Seal. Buy us a car."

Did Ivy League beauties do drugs? Wasn't there a political movement, what were they, libertarians, that wanted drugs to be legal? Were they fancy eggheads? God, why didn't he pay attention to this shit? He looked hard at Mara, trying to see past the beauty, the physical perfection, to the soul. Could he find that, when he didn't even know where his own was?

...

He bought a Camaro. It was green, mostly, with a few rust spots that it didn't get in the desert. It still had Florida plates. That, and the engine, a 350, were the deciding factors in his choice, along with the AM-FM cassette player.

The heat put moisture under his arms, but the bright flowers on his shirt didn't show it. A strand of hair came loose from its anchoring mousse at the top of his head and exposed a glistening piece of sweating scalp. Desert dry heat my ass, he thought. Heat is heat.

Progression normal, he decided, threading his steps through the sidewalk maze. *From Bond to gut-wrenching, next step dirty.*

Shave and a haircut, two bits.

Mara opened the door, and he almost forgot how afraid he was. She wore jeans and running shoes and a plain tee shirt in pale green, like her eyes. She had pulled back her hair as usual and tied it with a large bow that matched the t-shirt. Her shirt was not tucked in, he knew, because it had to cover the Glock 19 she wore in an inside holster. She always packed. He never did. That stuff was for subordinates who did the actual nabbing of the bad guys.

"Take your shirt off," she said, "and put this on." She was holding a shoulder rig. "I'll help you adjust it. That shirt is perfect, it'll go over it just fine."

"What is this?" he asked, as she fiddled with the buckles. "It looks like a Makarov."

"Sorry, I didn't tell you to bring yours."

"I dunno if I could even find mine, honey. What am I supposed to be doing with a Makarov?"

"You'll need one. It's his, but I'm not going to let him hold it just now."

"Him?"

"Yes. Come and help me get him to the car. I think it's dark enough outside."

She led him to the bedroom at the back of the apartment. When she turned on the light, he could see a rumpled pile, roughly human, on the bed.

"My god, that's Pavlenko," he said when the pile moved.

"Americans are so astute," said the voice from the pile.

"Help me get him up, Seal."

Mara and Pavlenko babbled away in Russian as Seal helped him walk to the door. They were silent outside, getting into the car quickly, Pavlenko lying on the back seat, Mara sitting in front.

As Seal started the car and turned on the lights, he was so overjoyed that Columbian cartels were not his particular problem this night, that he forgot to worry about the possibility of treason.

SIX

When the elevator hit the top number, Seal put the plastic card Mara had given him into the slot. The elevator went higher. To the moon, Alice. Seal rocked back and forth, toes and heels, caught himself holding his hands behind his back. "Whatever you do," Mara had said, "Keep your hands where they can be seen." Of course, he knew that; didn't need reminding from some close-mouthed, secretive, maddeningly cool little slip of a girl.

The hotel elevator brought him to a tiled anteroom. The mirrored wall before him had no apparent doors or even buttons. He smoothed the hair over his right ear and wondered what to do. There was a buzzing sound. He pondered it. There it was again. Of course! He pushed on the glass in front of him. It swung inward on silent hinges. He stepped through into another anteroom, or maybe it was a continuation of the first one, with the same tile, and the glass wall, not mirrored on this side, behind him. In front of him stood a man with an AK-47 pointed at him.

"Where's Mara?" the man demanded. He made his point with the gun, holding it casually with one arm and swinging it at Seal's favorite flowered shirt. He was youngish, Seal decided, thirties, early? With brown hair and over-large brown eyes and over-long eyelashes. Mara's boyfriend? Did Mara have a boyfriend? If she did, this one would probably be a contender. Seal felt regret, not jealousy. There had been a time when he would have been a contender, too.

He babbled his name.

The man was not listening. "I know who the fuck you are," he said. "Weapon?" He rested the barrel against Seal's sternum.

Seal moved to retrieve the Makarov from under his shirt. The barrel pressed harder.

"Just point to it," said the man.

The formalities complete, Seal was shown into a sumptuous reception room in the penthouse suite of O'Malley's Casino in Reno. He was led down two wide marble steps, across a white Berber carpet, and through double doors into a dining room. Here, quiet luxury gave way to activity and the familiar (to Seal) mess of an intelligence operation. Three computers lined the buffet. A printer buzzed on a trolley. An ugly African-American man wearing a shoulder holster and suspenders stood over it, reading the words as they spurted from the inkjet. The large table was strewn with documents and little Styrofoam coffee cups, some on their sides with brown rings around the inside bottoms. The table could seat twelve. It was meant for better things.

Only three men sat there, at the other end, a world away from Seal, their shirt sleeves rolled up, their ties loosened. They all wore guns in shoulder holsters. Seal recognized a Glock. Was that a SIG? His eyes stopped on this one, on the blue, blue irises that halted his gaze mid-sweep. He sensed, rather than saw, the third man, with dark somewhat wavy hair and dark eyes, to the left. This one, though, the one looking through him, old blue eyes here, was familiar. He remembered.

"Let us dispense with introductions since we know each other," said Mack. "Where is Mara?"

Seal swallowed. His jaw worked, but no sound came out. He knew he looked like Ralph Kramden in front of the boss. Did this guy know *The Honeymooners*? What a stupid question to be asking himself now.

He worked at it a little more. The dark-haired man tapped the table in front of him with a pencil. "She's at a motel," Seal managed. "Not too far. She said she had to change. The guy threw up on her. Just like a Russian, he had to have pickled herring, he said, and vodka. Well, we couldn't get no herring, so we got oysters. And Mara wouldn't let him have no vodka, on account of his condition, so she picked up a bottle of table wine, she said. But when she got back to the car, it turns out it was Boone's Farm Apple. I don't blame the guy for being sick. Mara just don't know these things; I try to teach her."

"Which motel?"

"I don't know. I can take you there. We need help getting him up here. He's pretty bad. He needs a doctor, too. He's got a bullet somewhere in here." Seal waved the flat of his hand vaguely around his abdomen, never taking his eyes off the man with the SIG.

Mack looked at the man by the printer. "Jay, can you bring us a doctor?"

The man tilted his heavy head forward, affirmative. "Listen, may I advise?" He waited. There was no objection. "I'd like to bring a babysitter, too. Things are becoming awkward for me. I will have to get back to Chicago." He ripped a string of pages off the tractor feed, waved them, pointed at them as if they might be read, as though the damp ink on them could float over the table for better communication.

"What babysitter?"

"Frank Cardova."

"He is on the East Coast."

"I took the liberty of having him come with me to Reno when you called. Something is up. I think we'll need him. I know it has been a long time since you worked with him, but there is a sea change here, and he is an experienced mariner."

...

Mara wore a white and navy nautical outfit, with a little white pleated skirt, blouse trimmed in navy, and little blue low-heeled pumps. Her hair was French braided, with a large navy-blue bow at the end. She did not belong in the dirty little motel room. Her perfume mixed with, and was overcome by, the stench of vomit and blood. It was this vision of a perfect rose on a battlefield that first mesmerized Seal and the two men who had come with him, Charlie, the younger blond man with the Glock, and Steve, the brown-eyed man he'd first met.

Something moved on the bed, breaking the spell. Pavlenko tried to sit up straighter against the headboard, his shirt front stiff with vomited blood and oysters and Boone's Farm. He wanted to stand, maybe, to face these two. Seal was aware they were enemies, but he was not prepared for the hopeless fear in Pavlenko's eyes as Charlie and Steve stepped toward him. The Russian tried to shield himself, feebly, at first.

Seal could see there was no defense, against the blows, against the sickening sound of them, against the conflict between being glad it wasn't him and wishing it would stop before he, too, threw up. He looked at Mara for relief, for an oasis, for a return to sanity. He could comfort her, protect her, lessen the ugliness for her by turning her pretty head aside. He was not needed. She was as emotionless as ever, as unimpressed by the hand-to-hand killing of a man as by the passing of a secret document.

Seal was sure he was going to throw up.

Pavlenko fell at Mara's feet. Steve raised his foot for another of those blows not seen, a species of kick Seal knew happened only by its effect on the body of the man on the floor. You never actually saw those kicks coming, did you? Mara placed a dainty, well-manicured hand on Steve's forearm and it stopped. Seal kept his dinner. Pavlenko caught his breath and spit out three teeth. Mara picked up the bloody teeth, and put them in her handkerchief, while Charlie and Steve carried him to the car.

On the way back to O'Mally's, Seal stopped the shaking in his hands by squeezing the wheel.

Mara sat next to him, saying nothing except, "Michael, stop it."

"I am not doing anything," came Charlie's voice from the back seat. "And my game name is Charlie. And this is Steve."

"Oh." She paused. "Should I have a game name? Stop hurting him; I can hear the changes in his breathing; you will kill him."

"Your father never used one. His name was an advantage, but not to you, Mara. Papa will send you straight home, no matter how cute you look. It does not matter if I kill this insect."

"Yes, it does. I have given my word to help him. Stop it."

SEVEN

John Fairfax put his right hand in his pocket while he walked through the parking lot of O'Malley's Resort and Casino. His left hand carried his call bag, with the instruments.

"Doctor Fairfax," said the short, fat man named Frank who walked beside him, "have you ever been out before?"

"No."

"May I suggest that you always keep your hands in the open, where they can be seen?"

That was the sum of their conversation. The FBI agent, Jay Turner, said nothing after the initial introduction. He put a forefinger in front of his large, ugly face and then pointed to the car whispering, "Not secure."

John had just finished a busy shift on call, with two appendectomies and a knife wound to the kidney. He did not relish earning the past year's worth of standby stipends from the FBI on this particular

night. The pay would triple, though, since he was being called out and that was good for all those out-
standing student loans. And you never knew, the case
might be interesting. Still, he had seen enough ordinary gunshot wounds not to count on it, though the
secrecy added some interest. Both these men, the ugly
one and the older, hairless fat man seemed serious
about their business.

The penthouse apartment they took him to was
like any other, except for all the guns, and the man,
his patient, bleeding on the Berber, and the beautiful
girl in a blue and white sailor dress trying to help the
bleeding man up while she argued in the most en-
chanting French. She argued with a tall, dark-haired
man who had just kicked John's patient in the ribs.
John heard the crack as he walked into the room. He
stood on a marble step between the FBI man, Jay, and
the bald one, Frank, and watched.

The patient crawled to a spot in front of someone
obviously in charge, also in his shirtsleeves and wearing a gun in a shoulder apparatus that looked uncomfortable. This man was about John's height, blond and
blue-eyed like him, too, but much older, though not as
old as his father. Late forties, maybe.

"Jay Turner has only English," said the man. He
had a heavy, German accent. This was shaping up like
a war flick. "Do you speak English, Sergei Nickolaevich?"

The patient did not answer but swayed on his hands and knees, which was as far as he had gotten toward a standing position.

"He speaks English." The girl answered for him. She did not have an accent, but why did she seem foreign?

The patient made it to his knees, looking at the blond man in front of him briefly, before he fell forward again and caught his fall with his hands. John stepped forward off the step. Frank held him back.

"What do you have for us?" the blond man asked the patient.

"When... we... get... there."

"Where?"

"Allow me to guess," interrupted Jay Turner. "To San Antonio. Am I correct?"

The patient nodded and wheezed.

"The whole world is going to San Antonio," explained the FBI man. "Every spook known to man or computer is there or is headed there. We have been instructed to let them all in and search any coming out. All documents are to be sealed and sent forward."

"If I may interrupt," said Frank. "Am I correct that this is Sergei Pavlenko? It's hard to tell."

A fat man in a loud shirt nodded at Frank.

"Just before Jay here contacted me," said Frank, "I was given a commission against Pavlenko." He looked at the pitiful lump on the floor. Everybody looked at it.

"Why?" asked the blond man.

Frank shrugged. "I was not privy to that information, Mack. I am authorized to offer twenty million." He took his eyes off Pavlenko and looked at the man he called Mack.

"Are you offering me the commission?"

Frank hesitated. "It's been so long and there is no verification this time. It has been getting bad lately, but this is the worst. I think it was assumed that we would use People's Fist for this one."

Mack's eyebrows rose, amazed. "People's Fist? They are Eastern."

"Yes," said Frank. "Like I said, things are, shall we say, different. If you want the commission, you can have it, for the full amount. The man is unarmed."

"Is this all your people want? Just the body?"

"And any documents he has on him. They should be sealed and sent directly up the chain."

"No questioning?"

"No. And no sign of torture. I might have to deduct for the teeth."

"Hah! You said full amount!" This came from the tall rib-kicker. The accent was French.

Mack held up one hand for silence. The patient, the Russian, whom they called Pavlenko, still swayed on his knees, supported by his hands, panting and wheezing like an injured dog. Mack looked down at him. "It is an enormous sum for one corpse. What is this document they want so badly, Sergei Nickolae-vich?"

The Russian did not answer right away. The room became completely silent when he finally spoke, and even then it was difficult to hear him. Several words were lost in his noisy efforts to breathe. "I... with... Semianov... died."

"You were with Semianov when he died?" asked Mack.

A painful nod, then, "I... three others."

"You and three others. Where are they?"

"Dead."

The Frenchman took his gun out of its holster and pointed it at the patient. "Let him join them, I say. Then we can collect Frank's commission and go home."

No one moved. Mack looked at each man in the room in turn, as if taking a poll. His gaze swept over John on its way to Jay Turner. Then he looked at the girl for what seemed a long time.

Finally, she said simply, "I gave my word that I would help him."

EIGHT

"Is this the doctor?"

The man gazed at him with an unpleasant, cold, and invasive examination of the soul, probing and

measuring John with pinpoint accuracy. Acutely uncomfortable, John swallowed hard.

Jay nodded.

They laid the patient on a large mahogany table
in the dining room, or what would be the dining
room if it were not full of computers and empty coffee
cups. The patient's belt scratched the finish as they
slid him into position, more or less centered at the far
end.

John opened his bag and looked for a place to lay
out his instruments. Someone moved a printer, and
the girl trundled the trolley it had been on to his side.
She laid a clean tea towel on top. He set out his instruments, still in their wrappers, freshly autoclaved.
She helped him put on his surgical gloves. He turned
toward the patient, whose shirt was already cut off.
Across the table, the Frenchman, the one who had
been ready to shoot the man, had taken his call bag
and begun the IV. He was already hanging a bag of
fluids, even though John gave no order. No, the
Frenchman told him, there were no drugs, nor anesthetic. Proceed, he said.

John was sure he had something in his bag. He
was already sterile and was about to ask them to look
again when a brown-eyed man in his thirties, the one
they were calling Steve, opened a wicked-looking
street knife with his thumb, roughly cut off a length of
Pavlenko's belt and shoved it in the patient's mouth
for a gag. He did not put away the knife, but let it

hang there in the air, pointed in John's direction. The dying man bit down hard and closed his eyes.

"Proceed," repeated the Frenchman.

Steve pushed past John to the other end of the table to hold the patient's legs. John gave him a sharp jab with his elbow as he passed. He decided he disliked Steve. He did not like the violence in his eyes and his manner and he despised the way the man looked at this girl. John already considered her his own, by the way she anticipated his every order. Steve could take a hike.

"Are you a nurse?" he asked her.

"No." She smiled a half-smile, melancholy. "I grew up doing this. I always helped the doctor when they came home."

"That is true. Masha sewed me up after the last time we met you, Sergei Nickolaevich." This came from the younger blond man who now positioned himself at the patient's head. "You remember Tbilisi, don't you? My leg was broken, and you made me stand on it. The doctor was not sure he would save it, but with Masha's help...." He jabbed a fist into the patient's broken ribs.

"Mara's help will be of no use to Sergei now," said the Frenchman, who held down the IV arm and the far hip. "This doctor is too young to finish secondary school."

His remark seemed directed at the round man who had brought him here.

John paused, the scalpel ready over the wound, while Mara swabbed again. Steve and the blond one —Mara called him Charlie—held the patient's legs and shoulders. Jay Turner took the near arm.

"I don't have time to list my awards," said John, "but I became a fully qualified forensic surgeon before age thirty, board-certified, and I graduated summa cum laude from the best medical school in the country."

"A typical American braggart," said the Frenchman.

John looked into the dark brown, almost black, eyes of the older man across the table from him and involuntarily shuddered. "I am trying to put the patient at ease," he said through clenched teeth.

Ha ha ha! All around the table. Even the girl smiled. Steve's laugh was the loudest. John already knew what he thought of that one. The patient began to sweat.

John worked quickly, did the minimum. Enough to stop the bleeding, repair the diaphragm, disinfect, and suture. The Frenchman came up with antibiotics from somewhere and administered them, again, before John could order it. The last straw, though, came as John pulled the final suture tight. From nowhere, the Frenchman drew out a bottle of morphine, measured, and gave the dose. The patient relaxed. Charlie pulled the leather gag from between his bleeding gums.

John faced the Frenchman across the table, scissors still in his hand. "Are you a doctor?" he demanded. He did not wait for any reply. "This is my patient. I order the meds. You said there was nothing here for pain. You are a liar." He pointed with the scissors to give his accusation emphasis.

John remembered the Frenchman vaulting over the table so fast he could only know of it by memory as he lay on the floor on the other side. Breath was also history; there was none in his body. He felt himself lifted off the floor, saw the fist headed for his eye, felt the impact, fist then wall. Pain registered. He thought only, oh god, please not my hands.

He heard a foreign voice, Mack's voice, and for a moment he saw himself on his hands and knees on a white Berber carpet; no, that was the patient. He was on his back against a wall, under a chair, everything looking pink, and his face was wet.

The voice said, "Do not kill the doctor, Louis," softly, indifferently, as in, I'll have my fish sautéed, not broiled.

Another voice, American with a soft Southern accent: "Just break his hands." This one was venomous, not indifferent. Had to be Steve. John rallied briefly, managed a breath, raised an arm to fend off the chair, and was lifted again against the wall, with one arm twisted and great pressure on his throat.

He looked into the dark eyes of a man of violence. The twisted arm turned again and he winced, saw amusement in those eyes. He tried to look defiant, another twist, an involuntary gasp, and the Frenchman smiled.

"You are summa cum laude from the College of Fools, Doctor, if you insult a man you cannot fight."

With great effort, he stayed standing when he was let go. The wall helped. It gave support. The girl helped. She was watching, giving him incentive to not crumple in front of her. Steve helped the most. His grin hit the other eye, the one not swollen, with triumph. John stood by force of will.

He had three great comforts. First, his hands were undamaged. Second, the girl did not gush over him, but only handed him a handkerchief. He thought at first it was to wipe the blood from the cut over his eye, but there was something in it. He opened it without shaking much and found three bloody teeth. It puzzled him at first; he had not lost any teeth; then he remembered. She had a bowl of disinfectant ready. He cleaned the teeth and put them back in the patient's mouth. There was some wire in his bag; he made a makeshift brace and while he fitted it, Mack provided the third comfort.

"So you think he will live," said Mack, not asking, just reading his mind. "When will you allow him to speak to us?"

It could only have been sweeter if the Frenchman himself had said, 'You are the doctor here.'

"Oh, by morning. Certainly, by morning."

NINE

I n the absence of any guidance, in the universal lack of deference to him as a surgeon and the presence of actual hostility from Steve and the Frenchman, John stayed in the dining room with his patient. It seemed the safest thing to do. The girl stayed, too. John admitted to himself, privately, that this was his real reason for staying.

When everyone else left the room, she cleaned the cut over his eye. She said, "Please be careful around Louis, Doctor. He can be dangerous with strangers. He is much more volatile here than he is at home."

"What's your name?"

"Mara."

"Mara. You speak beautiful French. Are you related to Louis? You said 'at home.'"

She chuckled, and shook her head, amused. "My father was the explosives expert for the team."

"Was? Team?"

"He died ten years ago. This man killed him." She pointed to the patient with her chin as she cut a length of gauze to dress the superbly sutured wound.

John waited, confused.

"He relayed the order," she explained, "which carries a degree of responsibility. Don't you think? I am not talking about collective guilt, you understand. Sergei was directly in the decision-making chain, not merely attached to it. One can deny responsibility all the way to the trigger, can't one? And finish with the absurdity that the gun alone did the killing."

"Then Mack is not your father?"

The half-smile vanished. "He is my stepfather," she said.

"Step?"

"He is married to my mother."

"Oh. And so Charlie is …"

"My stepbrother." She clipped the words.

He wanted to ask about Steve, but as if summoned by the thought, the man walked in, shaved and dressed in a suit and tie. He took the chair next to John and sat there smirking at his swollen eye.

"Mara, why don't you get some rest now," said John. "Thank you for your help. You're quite an expert."

The quiet little smile, the one her eyes did not join in on, came back and she shook her head. She sat down in a chair on the other side of the table. The blood on her white dress had turned brown and much of her hair escaped the braid at the back, hanging down in fine gold wisps around her face. Her eyes streamed from lack of sleep, leaving a smudge of mascara on one cheek.

"Mara's not going anywhere tonight, or she will lose her project," said Steve.

"He'll be all right," John told her.

"No, he won't," said Steve.

"I will watch him," said John.

"You'll watch him die," said Steve, laughing as he continued, "You don't think you could stop me, do you? Or any of the others? How about Louis? Fend him off with a fucking scissors, or better yet, fling insults at him. Deadly."

Steve finished his laugh and spoke to Mara. "You should go home, Mara. It isn't just a matter of a few bumps and scrapes. Other things happen to us. You saw Louis. In twenty-four hours, it will take all three of us to pull him off the doctor here, and by that time, I won't want to. Not that I'm all that motivated now."

"I have never known you to be such a bully, Steve," said Mara. She yawned. "What makes you hate the doctor so much?"

"He's arrogant."

"So are you," said Mara.

Charlie came through the door, also dressed to go out. Behind him was the man in the loud shirt. This was a different loud shirt. This one was clean.

"I thought Frank was going with you," said Mara. "Why are you taking both babysitters?" She narrowed her eyes at Charlie. "You are going to look for women, aren't you?"

"Louis is looking for women," said Charlie. "Frank will stay with him. We'll keep Seal with us. Jane Jared is in the hotel. We're hoping to run into her."

"Of course, you hope so. You think you are God's benefit to women, don't you?"

The man in the flowered shirt cleared his throat. "Uh, Mara, you mean God's gift to women."

"Thank you, Seal." She smiled and turned back to Charlie. "Jane Jared is not good for you, Michael Joachim. You like her too much."

"My game name is Charlie, for the hundredth time, and this is business. You just go on protecting your KGB bastard and let me get on with my job."

John had almost two seconds alone with her when they left, enough time to turn in her direction and open his mouth before Mack came into the room carrying two large Styrofoam cups. John closed his mouth.

Mara nodded where she sat. Her mascara poured freely down her cheek as she fought to keep her eyes open.

"Go," Mack said to her. "Get some sleep."

She looked at him doubtfully, worried.

"I will not touch him," said Mack. After a pause: "If they return, I will not let them touch him." Another pause: "I give my word."

John thought this would be a good time to go, too. The patient was stable, and Mara was gone and maybe he might find her in another room.

"You stay here tonight, Doctor."

The weight of one hand pushed him back into the chair. One hand backed up by excessive physical conditioning, John decided. He noticed the corded muscles on a scarred forearm. The knuckles were also scarred and calloused. The man took the next chair, turned it to face him and the door behind him, and sat down, within an arm's reach. He pushed one of the Styrofoam cups along the table toward John. "Coffee," he said. He took a sip from the other one.

The coffee was black and vile, but John drank it gratefully while he studied Mack.

Mack, of course, studied him back, with blue eyes in a faintly scarred face. Another scar, long and nasty, ran from the man's right ear to below the shirt collar. He wore his hair longer than his son did, and at the temples, the blond color had turned a more transparent gray. He wore a white shirt with the sleeves rolled up, no tie, top button open. Thick leather straps ran vertically down from his shoulders on either side. From one of these hung what John considered to be an enormous gun in a holster, from the other, a couple of long leather pouches.

John addressed the gun at first, forced himself to look into the blue eyes, then back to the gun. It seemed safer. "You are not an American," he said to the gun.

"No. I am Austrian."

"But Mara is American."

"Her mother is. Her father was Polish."

John forced himself to confront the eyes. "Charlie's English is very good."

"My wife, Mara's mother, taught him. He is very good at languages. I am not. I speak only a few."

John wondered. "I speak French," he said finally. "My mother is French Canadian."

"Yes. I know. You are from Baltimore, Maryland. Your family is wealthy, Catholic, and long established there. You have quarreled with your father and are paying for your medical training on your own. Jay gave me your file. I read it."

John did not know how to answer this.

"I suppose it is some distinction in this country to have two languages," said Mack. "Since many Americans cannot even manage one. I have difficulty, sometimes, deciphering the series of grunts and gestures that some pretend is English."

This was not exactly what John had been taught to consider polite conversation. He concentrated on his coffee. After five minutes of silence and a few more gulps of caffeine, he felt better and tried again, out of curiosity.

"What kind of gun is that?"

"It is a SIG-Sauer P226. I have had modifications made." Mack took it out of the holster, pulled back the slide, and pointed to something he called a compensator. "It helps to control recoil," he explained.

"Have you ever actually used it?"

Mack stared at him.

"So, all that stuff Frank said about twenty million for this guy's body is true? Are you a hitman or something?"

"Hitman?"

"Assassin. Killer. That kind of thing." Why the hell was he asking this? What answer was he looking for?

"Yes. Assassin is close."

"No kidding? And you work for Uncle Sam?"

"When he pays us."

"And Mara?"

"What about Mara?"

"She is an American."

"Mara only thinks she is American," said Mack. "She grew up in Europe and has no concept of how life is lived in this country. We thought her boss, Seal, would help in his peasant way, but he treats her like a fine crystal goblet, standing back to admire but doing nothing about the contents. I do not know what to do about her. I should send her home in the morning."

"Yes, you should." It was the patient who spoke.

John jumped up, grabbed for a pulse, and checked the eyes.

"Send her home. It occurs to me thith ith a trap," Pavlenko lisped through his wire brace.

"Such things usually are," said Mack. "But how should I send her? Shall I have her bound and gagged? Lock her in a dungeon? I cannot risk open defiance from her. In this family it is deadly, I have learned. Or perhaps that is your plan?"

"I swear to you I had nothing to do with it." The patient showed signs of distress. "Slavin was my boss. He told me to work with Jared. I thought we were going to trap you. I was not informed, and I protested when your wife was killed, and your little girl. I am so sorry. I was reprimanded. It is in my personnel file." He lifted himself on his left elbow to look at Mack.

John pushed him back down. Mack stood, walked to the buffet, and opened a drawer. Pavlenko continued to talk.

"Semianov told us, me, to give it to our enemies. The others tried and were killed. They were sold. There is no honor anywhere. You are the only honorable enemy left."

"What is it he told you to give me?" Mack took a metal box from the drawer.

"The file. The complete file. All of it." The patient was sweating. The pupils had dilated. "The list of all his work in this country. He ran the illegals and the agents of influence."

"Yes, I know. And why did he want his enemy to have it?" Mack handed the box to John.

"So that someone would appreciate the completeness of our victory."

"I have always known about your victory here, and I do not much care."

"Mara cares. I don't want her to be hurt. You must protect her."

Mack looked at the ceiling. John looked in the box. It held some disposable syringes and a row of morphine bottles. He took one of each and drew up a dose.

"All the roads open to me are perilous, Sergei Nickolaevich," said Mack. "If I send her home, she will defy me. Now that she has rescued you, she is in the game on a new level. People will think she is operational, and she will become a target. If she responds as she has been trained, she becomes a killer. Which do you recommend?"

John prepped Pavlenko's arm. Mack held up one hand. Wait.

"It does not have to go on," Pavlenko said finally.

"In my world—in the state of nature—it does. She is a third-generation Sobieski who has had two years, seven months of freedom. She is not twenty-two. Do you want to tell her she can leave the dungeon only if she kills? Do you want to show her the difference now that you have crossed that threshold?"

"I am truly sorry," the patient wheezed. "I did not understand. I had not yet crossed it when I asked for her help."

"You are sorry." It was a dead statement.

Mack nodded and John administered the dose. Pavlenko drifted back into unconsciousness.

John asked Mack one more thing before the others came in.

"You will court her whatever I say," was Mack's answer. "As long as you do not touch her, I will not stop you. Neither will I protect you."

TEN

Seal attacked the trolley when Jay wheeled it into the dining room. He took a bread roll off the top before Jay brought it to a stop. He had it buttered before Jay sat down at the table next to Frank. He had never been so hungry. He was glad to see this dawn and the breakfast that came with it.

"Is that blood on the table?" asked Jay.

"Where?"

"In front of you, where the crumbs are falling."

Seal shrugged.

Jay looked around the room. "Why is there blood on the wall?"

"Oh, that's the doctor's." Seal spewed bread-crumbs over a wide area.

The doctor came into the room. Jay studied his shiner and the gash above it, noticed the man's seedy condition. Jay had not slept that night either, but he had been able to shave. These three were not shaved.

The doctor was a mess, like the dining room, spattered with dried blood. Like Seal, he demolished a bread roll before collapsing into a chair at the head of the table.

"I leave you for a few hours thinking all is well," Jay said to Frank. "The team is in the capable hands of not one but two babysitters, and you guys let them beat up my doctor."

"What's a babysitter?" asked John.

"We are," said Frank. "We keep order, arrange logistics, try to avert disaster, that sort of thing."

"For the FBI?"

"No, no. We're not FBI. Jay is FBI, anti-terror. He's been the team's de facto babysitter for the past few years because of some strained relations, but we're the trained babysitters, though Seal hasn't worked in the field lately. Pavlenko's a babysitter, too, for the Other Side, or what used to be the Other Side."

"Not anymore," said Jay. "He has graduated."

Frank handed out Styrofoam cups. "I suppose if you define a specialist in terms of how many people want to kill him versus how many he has killed, then Pavlenko qualifies now."

"He is fully qualified," said Jay. He lifted an ornate china pot from the trolley. "I told them I wanted coffee. These look like teapots. Wait, it is coffee. Anybody?" Everybody. He poured. "Pavlenko killed two last night in California—probably the two who put that bullet in him. The message came into the Reno office this morning. I happened to be there to see it. Where is Charlemagne, by the way? Charlie met me at the elevator."

"Charlemagne?" asked John.

"The team. It's the name of the team," explained Frank. He turned back to Jay. "They're showering and changing. They had what they called a semi-workout on the covered terrace. They must've thought we were all asleep." He waived vaguely at Seal and the doctor to define all. "We hid behind the double screen by the piano. Even Pavlenko joined us when he could sit up. I'd have had popcorn for everybody, but the crunching would give us away. As it was, Pavlenko's gasping nearly tubed us a couple of times."

"Mack knew we were there, Frank," said Seal.

"Of course he did. He knows everything. He allowed it. Don't ask me why." He blew on his coffee.

"So a specialist kills people but a babysitter doesn't? Am I right?" asked John, trying to understand. "And because Pavlenko killed somebody, he's now the one and no longer the other? Is that what Mack meant about crossing the threshold?"

"Mack?" Frank looked at the doctor, puzzled. "Let me piece this together for you. Yes, a specialist is capable of killing if it's necessary. And we don't normally employ them unless we think it's going to be necessary. A babysitter doesn't and mustn't do any actual killing but don't think that we deny responsibility."

"Yes, I understand that. Mara explained it."

"Mara?" Frank's normally bulging round eyes seemed ready to pop out of his head. "You've been discussing the game with Mack and Mara? They spoke to you about it? I want every word."

"Don't start that, Frank," said Jay. "I stuck my neck out to get you here. The rule is NO MORE FILES."

"I know. I know. After thirty years in the game, it's hard to break the habit. This morning's workout was incredible. I've never been this close."

"What was incredible?"

"The girl. The girl can fight, can't she?" Frank looked at Seal, who nodded. "She decked the Frenchman,"

"She what?"

"Laid him out, well, doubled him up, I should say. She kicked him in the groin. They were sparring."

Seal and John nodded. Witnesses.

Jay's heavy jaw fell open.

Frank continued, "She apologized and worried over him and when he could talk again he said don't worry about it but don't think you're so great until you can do that to Steve. The doc here translated for us. His French is not as rusty as mine. We were writing all this on paper so they wouldn't hear us whisper. I have it here somewhere."

"I'd burn it if I were you," said Jay. "Then what happened?"

"So then the Frenchman took over guard duty from Mack and they traded sparring partners until eventually it was Steve against Mara. She did very well at first but complained he was holding back, so Charlie told him to stop holding back. Well, Steve hit her square in the solar plexus with what they called a thrust-kick and she flew across the terrace and landed against the wall. I had to sit on the doctor here to stop him from getting himself—and maybe us—killed. Seal clamped both hands over his mouth. You have us to thank that he's even alive. He's done nothing but get himself in trouble since he got here."

"If Pavlenko's up walking around, I'd say he's done a little more than that," said Jay. "Who blacked his eye?"

"The Frenchman."

"Starting early, is he?"

"He's in a fine state," Frank replied.

"But it's Steve who's gonna kill your doctor, " said Seal.

ELEVEN

Mara smiled at the groggy, unshaven group at the table. She wore tight blue jeans and a plain brown T-shirt. The shirt was tucked in and the stock of her Glock 19 protruded from an inside holster on the front waistband of her jeans. She rummaged through the buffet and began setting out plates, forks, knives, cups, saucers, and finally, damask napkins. She wiped the blood and breadcrumbs off the table and set ten places.

Charlie stood in the doorway while the babysitters scrambled to get out of Mara's way. Sergei Pavlenko stood behind him, in borrowed clothes: a clean, red polo shirt and chino trousers.

Charlie waited for Mara to place the last fork, then said, "Now go change your clothes, Mara."

"You're not the boss of me, Michael Joachim," she said in a little girl's voice. She began to transfer serving dishes from the trolley to the table.

The babysitters and the doctor edged away. Charlie took a long time to reply.

"Yes, I am the boss of you, Mara. You have no status here. We are on an operation and my word is the same as Papa's. The same, Mara. Go change."

Seal sucked in his cheeks. After seven months he knew how best to get her to cooperate. This was not it. Mara's face showed surprise at first, then doubt, rebellion, and then it turned pale when Mack came in through the double doors, looking very distinguished, Seal would say, in a three-piece suit like something out of a rich people's catalogue. He had shaved and was alert enough, though, like the rest of them, he had not slept that night. He brushed past the Russian and Charlie and stopped in front of Mara. There were no words. Mara blushed, then walked quickly out of the room. When she came back, she was wearing a skirt and blouse, in a pink knit, that covered the Glock and matched the ribbon around her ponytail.

She took the seat at the opposite end of the table from Mack and played hostess like she was born to it, with the doc to her left and Steve on her right, glaring at each other across the table. Charlie sat on his father's right, Louie at Mack's left. Sergei and Seal took seats between the doctor and Charlie, and across from them sat Jay and Frank.

Jay started talking first before a piece of toast was buttered.

"I cannot get your jet into San Antonio," he told Mack. "I am under surveillance myself. There is a lawyer from the justice department on my tail and she's been given my best special agent as an assistant."

"I know," said Steve. "We saw Roger last night. Is this lawyer's name Judy something or other?"

"Simons," said Jay. "That's the one. Disconcertingly serious and sensible. Worst nightmare. I can see you have met her."

"I told Roger we were here to discuss a proposal from Frank," said Steve. He looked at Mack. "I left out the details."

"You were too busy fending off the lawyer," said Charlie. He put his knife and fork down, sat back in his chair, and smirked down the table at Steve.

"That was one of the longest hours of my life," said Steve. "I thought you'd never finish with that girl. I still say she's dirty, Charlie. Why don't we ask the Russian?" He looked at Sergei. "Jane Jared. Is she in the game?"

"Who? Eben Jared's daughter?" Pavlenko winced as he sat up straighter. "Her mother is."

"That is not possible," said Jay. "We cleared her many years ago."

"She runs a cell of illegals. One of them is the man in your organization who cleared her."

"Who?" demanded Jay.

Pavlenko shrugged. "I don't know. It is on Semianov's list. I did not have access." He put a forkful of scrambled eggs in his mouth.

"But the girl," insisted Steve. "Is she dirty?"

"She's not, Steve, she..." Charlie was interrupted by his sister.

"Jane Jared?" Mara asked. "I told you when you danced with her at my graduation that she's in the game, Charlie."

"No, she's not, Mara. She is only misguided. A true believer who thinks she will save the world. She told me how she nearly had you expelled over that party of yours. She regrets being so overzealous."

"She's in the game," insisted Mara. "She knows all the tradecraft and practiced it flawlessly in school."

"She is the daughter of a specialist, for heaven's sake. What do you expect?"

Sergei used a piece of bread to clean his plate. He was still chewing when he spoke. "I think Masha is correct."

"Verify it, Pavlenko." There was heat in Charlie's words.

"I cannot. I did not have access. I can only tell you two things. First, you know that I was trained by Eben Jared. But I am not a specialist."

"Was," muttered Steve.

Sergei paused and nodded. "Was. I was not a specialist, but at the time I entered the directorate, we had lost so many babysitters, that it was decided we should be trained just as well as the specialists. It was thought that babysitters were dying because they could not defend themselves."

"No thought ever given to ordinary incompetence?" Frank rolled his round eyes to the ceiling.

Sergei shrugged. "My section commissioned Jared to train me and another man. During our training, one time, I made a mistake."

"Only once?" Steve asked with one eyebrow raised.

"Only once." Sergei glowered at him. "I do not recall what I did, but I remember what Jared said to me. He said, 'I know a little girl who can do that better than you.' This was about twelve years ago. Jane Jared is how old now, twenty-two?"

Mara nodded.

Charlie said: "So she was trained to defend herself. That does not mean she is operational."

"What is the second thing?" asked Mack.

Sergei winced. He shifted sideways, then sat straight against the back of his seat. He pulled at the bandage around his abdomen and ribs.

"Go lie down," the doctor told him.

Sergei waved him off impatiently.

"You are in pain," insisted the doctor.

"But not from the wound," whispered Sergei. He pushed his chair away from the table. The doctor was the only person in the room who did not recognize a defensive posture.

When Sergei spoke, finally, his words came at a steady, measured pace, while his eyes swept the room, pausing, in turn, to study Steve Donovan, the Frenchman, Mack, and Charlie, in turn, continuously.

"Last year," he said, "I attended a special course at Moscow University with the other man who trained with me under Jared. We learned the language of the new politics. When we finished, we received our assignments."

He took a deep breath, then plunged. "I was assigned to Mara. She had recently graduated from her college. My orders were to watch her until she became operational and then attempt to recruit her. If she declined, I was to kill her immediately."

Mara's right hand rested gently on Steve's shoulder. He stayed in place and so did the other three specialists. Sergei still held the edge of the table, prepared to use it as a springboard, only waiting for the first sign to figure out which way he should run.

TWELVE

"That's pretty stupid. You must have some real idiots in charge over there." It was Seal who broke the silence and relieved the tension all at once. He was still eating. The words came through a mouthful of sausage.

"Yes." Sergei sighed.

"Stupid?" demanded John. "You mean evil!"

Seal's fork paused a few inches from his face. He frowned. "No. Stupid. Evil in relation to what? Pavlenko was a babysitter. It was goofy to expect him to kill like that. Impossible. I know."

"I don't understand."

"What he means, Doctor," said Frank, "Is that such a killing requires a specialist. A babysitter doesn't have the right psychology. Pavlenko's superiors should have known that."

"They did not," said Sergei. "Seal is correct. They were idiots. My new boss has never met a specialist."

"I still don't understand," muttered John. He looked up in surprise when Frank spoke again. He did not expect an explanation from these people.

"When you practiced your cut and sew techniques on our Russian buddy here last night, what were you thinking, Doctor?"

John squinted with one good eye. "Thinking? I don't think; I just do. I concentrate."

"You blot out, however briefly, the fact that this is a human being under your knife. It is a clinical skill, Doctor. Take away the Hippocratic prohibition against killing, add some physical training, and you could be a specialist. A babysitter, generally, could not, at least not just like that, especially with the commission being a beautiful young woman."

Mara blushed.

John was dumbfounded. He looked at Mack. "Does this mean that you could?"

"Could what?"

"Kill a young woman?"

"That was not Sergei's order."

"It was."

"No. The order was to kill an operational enemy specialist. Any specialist can do that."

"Then you're saying you'll kill anybody for money?" John's tone became belligerent. He could not scrub it clean. He waited while Mack eyed him thoughtfully.

"I said nothing of the kind," Mack replied. "Tell me, Doctor. Do you remove any organ for money?"

"Of course not. It has to be diseased. I run tests."

Mack inclined his head and raised an eyebrow. Point. He focused again on the squirming Sergei and cleared his throat.

"You were telling us about the course you attended with Maximovich."

Sergei stared at him a minute, then shook himself and shrugged. "Yes. I attended with Maximovich. We both behaved ourselves long enough to graduate. Volodya and I celebrated with vodka. We had a long conversation that night."

"And you discussed your assignments?" asked Frank.

"We are never so unprofessional," insisted Sergei. "No. But we did talk about the question of which has more influence, heredity or environment?"

There was a long pause.

"That's it?" asked Charlie. "That's your second point?"

"I did not bring up the topic," said Sergei. "Volodya did."

"So?"

"So he also mentioned you in his argument, as an example of the power of heredity."

"It is natural for a babysitter to use a well-known specialist in his examples," said Frank.

"We had been shown a film of you that day, before receiving our certificates," said Sergei.

"What film?" asked Charlie.

"A new film, only a few days old, of a graduation ball in the United States. The film featured you, with still frames and closeups, dancing with a partner who was deliberately obscured. Her face was not shown."

Charlie did not answer.

"She had soft brown hair, in tight curls."

"Use the method, Charlie," said Mara. "Think."

"Be quiet, Mara."

"I will not be quiet. I will give you more to think about." She watched him roll his eyes at the ceiling. "I was awake last night when you and Steve came in. I listened, there, at the door." She pointed behind her. "I heard all of Steve's jokes about the ugly lawyer, and I am sure they were very funny, you all laughed so hard." She looked at Steve. "Did she really unbuckle your belt?"

Steve reddened. Mara did not wait for an answer. She spoke to her brother. "I know you think I am naive, but I have learned some things, and I can use the method as well as you can, and you know it. If Steve said that you opened the door to an adjoining room, a bedroom, and came out of it with Jane Jared, that means that you were first in it, and with the door closed. I know what that means." She wagged a finger at Charlie.

The expressions around the table were mixed wonder and amusement. Jay Turner did his best not to choke on the coffee he had just inhaled. Seal's mouth gaped open. Only John smiled openly at her, delighted.

Charlie suppressed a smile. "What does it mean, Mara?"

She opened her mouth to answer but closed it again on a warning look from Mack. "I do not know much," she said more humbly. "Stop laughing at me; I know you are." She kicked Steve.

"Ow!"

"I do not know much," she repeated. "But I know about women and after two years at school, I know Jane Jared. An ugly woman with no self-respect may run after Steve, but Jane Jared is very beautiful. She runs after no one. And she would not descend into bed," Mara paused, doubtful, and looked at Seal.

"Ah, I think it's 'hop' you want." He wiped at a smear of jelly on his shirt.

"Hop. She would not hop into bed with you without a purpose."

There was a low-level explosion in the room, coffee spewed, forks and knives hopping off the table as it was pounded, Frank's bald head shining crimson, and Louis's outright guffaw.

Spanish had been Seal's expertise, so he didn't catch Charlie's next words in German, but he knew a threat when he heard one. This one was lost in the noise. He looked across at Frank. Not lost entirely. Frank always had been a sponge. Seal was sorry, though, that nobody said 'you're right' to Mara, because, of course, she was, and what a waste that such a mind, essentially a male mind, though parts were feminine enough, should be packaged so deliciously, making people think it was a truffle, treat it like a truffle, when it was pure protein, prime beef grade-A, with language being the only problem. Her English was perfect, American, with absolutely no cultural content whatsoever.

Mara incorporated the oddest combination of traits he had ever met in a person. He suspected he was one of only a few people in the world who saw her as a person with traits as opposed to the other way around. He would have gone on thinking, but he felt Mack's blue eyes on him and when he glanced up, he saw that instinct had told him right. Mack's gaze was one of those that make you glad when it ends, and he hasn't shot you. Seal was glad accordingly.

Jay started talking again. He had one of the most pleasant listening voices ever made, deep and confident. You could crawl inside it and feel safe. The topic was enemies here and bad guys there, but everything was all right because Jay's voice was in charge. Seal felt himself nodding. There was a thud on the table. He forced his eyes open.

"What was that?" somebody asked.

"The doctor is asleep on his toast," somebody else replied.

Seal looked and it was true. The doctor's blond head was nestled on a plate of toast. There was butter on his nose. He snored through it. The meeting went on and on and on.

THIRTEEN

John Fairfax woke when the meeting was over because it was over. He could sleep on a gurney stuffed in a corner of the ER, on a desk at the nurses' station or a dining room table in a hotel penthouse, but he could not sleep without noise. Silence requires a comfortable bed.

He picked his head up off the plate, moved his stiff neck slowly, and thought he heard it creak. The room was silent. The people were gone; the computers, even the printer, had disappeared. The remains of breakfast were there, plates, cups, forks, knives, spoons, butter bowls, bread plates, crusts of rolls and toast and hash browned potatoes, spilled coffee in fine china saucers, overturned Styrofoam cups with more coffee, spilled and cold and forming map projections in sodden furniture wax on the table.

Gone? Mara, gone? She had to be gone. No woman he knew would allow such a mess to remain this long—he checked his watch—until afternoon. Gone, and in trouble? His addled impulse was to save her. He dashed into the hall and heard voices to his right. He followed the noise down the hallway, and heard a stereo or maybe a radio, playing Chopin. He came into the apartment living room, where last night he had watched the Frenchman break the patient's ribs.

And there she was, still in her pink knit outfit, playing a card game with three men at a small, square, table. Her back was to him. He lurked in the hallway, not feeling presentable. Pavlenko faced Mara on the other side of the table, playing as her partner, pale except where the bruising made him purple. The two babysitters sat at the other two sides of the little table. Frank nodded at him.

With Mara safe, the next great urgency presented itself. He tried the doorknobs along the hall.

"What do you need, Doctor?" Frank interrupted the game to help him.

"A toilet." Bad. He fought with the next doorknob and pushed his shoulder into the door.

Frank pulled him away. "I wouldn't do that, Doctor. Mack's asleep in there. Or was. Please stop trying to get yourself killed." He pointed down the hallway, past the kitchen. "Third door on the right. It's open.

And did you know you have a piece of toast stuck to your face?"

The bathroom held the same odd recipe of six-parts luxury to four-parts squalor. The room was large, tiled in white, with everything in it: a toilet, bidet, and marble shower, which dripped, and on the white tiled floor wet towels, t-shirts, a tie with regimental stripes—who wore that?— and pantyhose.

Toothbrushes, new ones in packages, various used ones, tubes of toothpaste, opened and not, disposable razors, and a large jar of aspirin littered the sink. John settled for four from the jar, though his headache demanded more. He sucked up water with his hand; there were no glasses. He brushed his teeth washed his face and decided he would shave when he got home.

There was precious little time between now and then to at least get her phone number. He ran into the hall and into Mack. It was like dashing himself against a wall.

"I am sorry," Mack said after he pushed John away. "Did Frank tell you that you must come with us to San Antonio?"

John wondered about telepathy. The news was good, at first, until he forced himself to remember where he was. He shook his head. No. He wanted to court her from the comfort of a normal life, even long distance, occasionally flying to—where did she live? —someplace, any place, away from Steve Donovan.

"We can take care of Pavlenko," said Mack.

Pavlenko? The patient. That's right, there is a patient. Take care of? As in?

"But Frank has told his section that we accepted the commission on him," Mack explained. "We will drive to San Antonio in what Jay Turner calls a recreational vehicle in order to hide him. If we let you go home now, I am afraid they will have it out of you in five minutes that he is alive and with us."

"I assure you, sir, that I won't tell a soul." John's voice trailed off under the steady strength of Mack's gaze. Telepathy came to his mind again, a peculiar kind of communication without words. "You don't mean they'd torture me, do you? My own government, or whatever they are? You're not serious? You are serious."

Mack pointed at one of the red-brown stains on John's sleeve. Pavlenko's? His own? Who knows. "This is not television, Doctor. You cannot turn it off."

The credits rolled to the sound of a piano. "Isn't that Litolff?" John asked as Mack moved past him. "What a brilliant recording!"

"That is not a recording. It is Charlie—on the piano, by the terrace."

John stood in the hallway, listening. This was not just good; it was genius. Genius wears a gun. Genius makes love to a woman his sister swears will kill him. Genius stands for hours on a broken leg. Genius beats up a man who once tortured him. A misplaced application of genius, buried by circumstance. Crowds will never hear this. Critics will never acclaim it. The man will die young by all indications. He will die never having been known or heard beyond this hallway and whatever little world these people crawl to when they're not doing… this.

Because 'this' is all there is outside of… John searched for a word to define what he considered himself to be in and this to be outside of, a word that would encompass law, art, road signs, and hospitals. Civilization. The uncomfortable suit of dress-up clothes that everybody wants to change. Make it new. Go back to something older. Change its fabric, its history, its weight, its style. Rip it apart and start over. Start over and this is what you get: cool slaughter, of geniuses and young women and of the sensibility that there is anything to be preserved in such people, not the least of which is the limit on their ferocities. He looked at his hands. What about a talented surgeon? Ditto diddly. That's what about. He'd be another blond cadaver. He hoped he wouldn't. He hoped he'd come home from San Antonio, he'd get the girl, live happily ever after, and tell his grandchildren about the adventure. His one adventure. He didn't want any more.

Litolff became Liszt. The mood depressed itself, synchronized with his own. A telepathic family for sure. He heard the bathroom door open, turned, and looked down the hall. Mack walked toward him, and in that walk, accompanied by the Second Hungarian Rhapsody, John knew more about the man than poor fat Frank had learned in decades.

"Are you all right, Doctor?"

John nodded. Mack went back into the bedroom to sleep again.

John found an uncomfortable ladder-back chair in the living room, moved it near the card table, and sat down to watch the game.

"There!" Mara threw a card down. "I have trumped over you!" she said to Frank.

"Ah, just trumped, or trumped it. You trumped the card, Mara," said Seal.

"Oh. I thought perhaps it was related to triumph."

Seal shrugged. "It's my trick, anyway." He put an ace of trump, in this case diamonds, on top of her ten.

She was incensed. "But I have not turned any tricks. I will lose the melds."

Seal gathered the cards toward himself. "Pulled tricks, honey, pulled. Prostitutes turn tricks. In Pinochle, we pull them. And it's meld. Just one for all the points, and anyway your partner has pulled a trick, so your meld is safe."

Sergei held up four cards to show her, though he did not seem at all confident of their meaning. They smiled at each other, in mutual triumph.

Mara frowned again. "Prostitutes play cards? Oh, hello, John. Frank and Seal are teaching us a card game. Do you want to play?"

Seal again: "No, he can't play. He would need a partner."

"We could wake Steve."

John shook his head. "No. No. I'll watch."

"It's your turn," Frank reminded her. After she put down a card he said, "So, Mara, do you mind if I ask, who is Udo Bitlerburg?"

"No." She went on looking at her cards, grinning and full of mischief. "You may ask."

It was Sergei who said finally. "So who is he?"

"The Baron von Bitlerburg? A completely odious man who must be forty at least, with no chin, moist hands, and a laugh like a donkey's bray. I danced with him once at a ball and Mi... Charlie has never let me hear the end of it." She threw down a queen, her last card.

Sergei said, "Charlie threatened to make sure you marry him."

John sat forward in his seat.

"The case is shut." She looked at Seal, brow furled.

"Closed. Case closed."

"Yes. It is." Then to Sergei: "Are you going to deal?"

He shuffled the cards and dealt. Mara picked up her cards one by one and arranged them thoughtfully. She looked up in response to the silence. Nobody else had picked up their cards. They all stared at her, waiting.

She sighed and put her cards down. "Babysitters are so nosy. You are like three little old busybodies. Four. You, too, John. I am not going to marry the Baron. Charlie was teasing, one of his nasty teases, but just a tease. When I finished that dance with Udo, he left me there. Right there on the ballroom floor." She swept over the table with a graceful gesture, making a ballroom floor out of it. "He marched then to Misha and did not ask, no, he demanded my hand."

It was Frank who managed to close his mouth long enough to ask, "What did Misha, uh, Mack, say?"

"I have not been told the exact words," she said. "But I understand that they were colorful and had to do with the Baron's ancestry, which in places is doubtful. But I think that Misha just wanted to squish him."

"Squish him?"

"Yes. Some say the Baron has Nazi sympathies. Misha despises Nazis."

"Worse than communists?"

"The same. He considers them the same."

"Squish him? How?" John asked.

Mara placed a manicured thumb on the table and rubbed. "Squish is a very descriptive word, don't you think?"

"But how?"

"He hoped the Baron would challenge him to a duel."

"A duel? With what? Pistols at dawn?"

"Sabers, of course."

"And Mack would win," said Frank. "Of course."

"Of course. But the Baron's friends were there, and they managed to clamp their hands over his mouth and drag him out. Later, he apologized to Misha. Case closed."

"*He* apologized?" Frank murmured.

But Mara picked up her cards again and gave the cold green stare that Seal translated, by mouthing it silently, as "case closed." Frank looked at his cards and began sorting them.

They played another hand of pinochle. Mara was an expert now, telling everybody what cards they held, winning decisively. Sergei supported her, grinning. He did not look right to John. Drugged, no doubt, with God knows what out of the Frenchman's stash.

The Frenchman breezed through the room once or twice, carrying a pouch of tools or a canvas bag that clanked. One of these times, after he left through the door to the elevator, Frank asked Mara, "How is Mildred, by the way? I have not heard from her in a long time."

"Mildred?" asked Seal.

"Louis's wife."

"Louis? Married?"

"To a former babysitter." This came from Sergei. Frank looked at him sharply.

"Mildred died last year," said Mara.

"I am sorry." Both American babysitters murmured.

"We were, too, in a way, but as these things go, it was peaceful. She died of cancer. It was more of a release for her. We are not accustomed to death from natural causes."

As if to remind John of the alternative, Steve Donovan entered the room from the hallway. At the same time, Charlie came in from the terrace. John noticed that everybody was well dressed, white cotton shirts and silk ties, summer-weight wool suits, gray for Charlie, a light brown for Steve. Steve's brown hair was combed. Frank's little bit of hair was also combed, a fresco around a dome. Even Seal wore a clean shirt, wrinkled and loud, but clean. It made John feel seedy, unkempt, unshaven. He was beginning to smell a bit. He knew the purple eye did not flatter his face.

Steve walked up behind him and jerked the chair out from under him. He was quickly on his feet again with his fist ready and heading for Steve's left brown eye, but his arm stopped well behind him. Momentum made him reel and upset the card table.

The patient, who was holding his arm, said, "Doctor, come and change my bandage."

John was not about to, but the Russian had a firm grip. John tried bringing his left arm over to break free, but this, too, was held—by Charlie.

"I can lend you a change of clothes," said Charlie.

What with flailing about and reeling across the carpet, the fact that he needed some cleaning up was pretty obvious, but John could not give Steve-the-jerk such an easy victory. He used his wits and settled down. He spoke reasonably. "In a minute. It's okay. I'm not a fool."

They released him slowly. Steve grinned and stepped closer.

John prepared to launch.

"How do you tell the difference," said Sergei, stepping between them, "between a brave man and a fool?"

Mack, Louis, and Jay Turner came into the room, adding to the circle standing around them.

"How *do* you tell the difference between a brave man and a fool?" said Jay.

Sergei stepped up to Mara, gathered her in his arms, and kissed her, for what seemed centuries. It must have been awkward, with one side of his mouth swollen and a wire holding his teeth in place.

Awkward or not, it sent John straight into the general fray, which eventually resolved itself into two piles: the specialist team, all of them: Mack, Louis, and Charlie, holding Steve; the babysitters, including Jay, holding the doctor.

Sergei held up one finger didactically. "The answer? The man who survives is a brave man. Come, Doctor, I need medical attention."

Mara's smile reminded John of the Mona Lisa.

FOURTEEN

S ergei pulled John down the hallway. Charlie followed them into a bedroom and locked the door behind them.

The room was meant to be splendid but was littered with assorted trunks, boxes, and canvas bags, some of them spilling their contents on the floor, one or two on the huge bed itself, which was rumpled but intact, with the pillows still covered by a chartreuse spread. Clothing had escaped most of the duffels, and crumpled or folded, was strewn everywhere, under, around, and next to black-painted equipment, flashlights, radios, ropes, and boxes of cartridges. Charlie handed John an olive-green bag filled with gauze, tape, and antibiotic creams. Sergei lay on the bed, pulling his shirt up and over the abdominal dressing, showing only an inch or two of the elastic bandaging that encased his ribs.

There was nothing wrong with the abdominal dressing, and anyway, John was not a nurse.

"Change the dressing, Doctor," said Charlie.

"You are a great challenge to babysitters, Doctor," said the patient. "I wonder if you will outlive me. You were busy making yourself into a fool, soon to be a dead fool."

"You kissed her." It was the only thing John could squeeze between his teeth as he removed a perfectly good dressing.

"Yes. It was painful but delicious."

Charlie rummaged in a suitcase.

"I will tell you a secret, though," said the Russian. "It was not brave or foolish. I knew they would pull him off me. Your reaction, I did not worry about, but Donovan's? I knew they would not let him kill me. When the time comes, there will be a decision. It is more likely to be Charlie here. Am I correct?"

Charlie held out another polo shirt like the one Sergei wore. This one was green. "Perhaps," he said.

"Perhaps?" John touched a betadine wipe to the edge of the wound. "Just like that?" He wiped the incision. It looked healthy. He admired the sutures, small, neat, and tight. A-plus work.

"He killed my mother and sister," said Charlie. "I have a claim."

"I did not! I did not know! I told your father last night. Slavin lied to me. I was part of the operation. I take responsibility for Sobieski, but I did not know the woman and girl were targets. I could not. Ekaterina, your mother, was my cousin. My bosses knew that. They said nothing to me. When it happened, I protested and was reprimanded. It is in my personnel file. I can show you. We are cousins. I do not kill women and children."

"Cousins, Pavlenko?" Charlie reached into another suitcase with a cool, controlled movement that reminded John of some of Mara's manners, precise, simple, and emotionless. Considering the topic, he wondered at it.

The patient pushed John's hand away where he had been swabbing distractedly.

"My father changed the name during the first purge, for survival, to a name from my mother's family. They were Ukrainian."

"Is survival all there is, Sergei Nickolaevich?" asked Charlie.

"You tell me, Mikhail Mikhailovich."

They stared at each other.

"The shirt should fit you, Doctor," Charlie said finally. "But trousers may be a problem; you're a little shorter than me. Steve's may fit you, though." He opened another green canvas bag.

John could not bear the thought and it registered on his face.

"Doctor, forget Mara," said the patient. "She is not for you. Too much cholesterol. She will clog your arteries, give you heart attacks." Pavlenko laughed and wheezed. He paused and became serious. "She is not for Steve Donovan, either if that will make you less of a danger to yourself."

John looked up sharply. "Why is that?"

"In addition to being as American and bourgeois as you are, he is also divorced. It will not do. He knows this."

"Then why?"

Charlie answered. "He despises your presumption, John. Sergei is right. Forget it. Steve is not an ordinary rival."

"Also, Doctor," said Sergei, "you must, very quickly, learn specialist psychology. I did not save your life just now because I think anything of you, grateful as I am for your work. It was my babysitter instinct. When the violence begins, anyone in the way, anyone who does not know what he is doing, is at risk. You may think right now everybody is only sitting around, but this is deceptive. The specialists are becoming more open to attack, and therefore more edgy. They are preparing to die and preparing to kill. The more you play with Donovan, the worse he becomes, harder to control, more difficult to predict."

"Play?" John concentrated on finding the beginning of a gauze roll. "Mara's an American and I'm not bourgeois."

"You are bourgeois. All Americans are bourgeois, even the rich ones, especially the rich ones because they are Puritans at heart. Mara only thinks she is an American. Her mother, Alex, left the country at age twenty. All she has is the language. Mara does not even have that. Listen to her taking lessons from Seal."

"How do you know about Steve's divorce?" Charlie asked Sergei.

Sergei shrugged.

"Do you know where they are?"

"The ex-wife and the boy? Yes. It was in the file. One of my subordinates found it while I was away. He was promoted and it was put in the file. I know everything about all of you, though I must admit I was not prepared for the Litolff. I knew you here," he pointed to his head, then to his heart, "not here."

"What file?" said Charlie. There was the same simple control again, making his voice flat.

John shivered involuntarily.

"I destroyed it," said Pavlenko. He motioned to John privately with his fingers, hurry up.

"Tell me about the file Sergei Nickolaevich."

The patient began to perspire. John tried to concentrate on folding the gauze.

"It had everything in it, even from your grandfather's day. Felix never destroyed anything, you know? But I did. I burned it."

"When?"

John laid the gauze on the wound.

"When?"

"In February."

"Next big question. Answer it well, Pavlenko. Well and completely. Why?"

John could not find the beginning edge of the surgical tape. Damn it. His patient's nervousness was affecting him.

"I went home for a visit. I destroyed it."

"Why, Pavlenko? You want me to ask you another way?"

"No. No. I went home to check the file. I needed to verify a theory of mine. I saw the new notation about Donovan's family and it bothered me, raised the ghosts of ten years ago, so I destroyed it."

"The whole file? For the one notation? Come on Pavlenko." Charlie threw down the pair of blue jeans he had been holding and took a step toward them.

John put the tape on crookedly.

Pavlenko held both hands up, just as Charlie grabbed his shirt at the front collar. The bandage dangled.

"It had been copied!" Pavlenko whispered hoarsely.

Charlie let go. The man fell back on the bed. John tore off another strip of tape.

"My alarms were tripped, all of them. I could tell it had been tampered with, and I have a chemical that will tell me when a document is photocopied. I destroyed the whole thing in the incinerator downstairs. Then I went to see Semianov. He was dying in a hospital in Siberia. He said he had been waiting for me. He said he copied it for insurance, to make Charlemagne want the file. It is with his list of illegals."

"Then this is a trap." Again, simple, flat, control.

"Among other things. But there is no choice."

"We can move the woman and boy."

"But she is difficult," said Pavlenko. "She is a typical bourgeois American for whom the world is a benign place, one who is offended by storms and earthquakes and thinks the president is at fault. The fuss she made the last time you moved them is what drew my subordinate's attention. Every time you move her you only renew interest. Better to get the file and destroy it."

Charlie stood silent for a long time. Long enough for John to place three more crooked strips of tape.

"You did not tell my father about this file."

"No. I did not have to tell him. He knew, somehow."

"What else is in it?"

"I did not have to tell him that, either. Everything in his file that describes him is accurate, you know. He understands without words. Amazing."

"What else?" Charlie held him by the shirt again.

"Let me explain that I am not stupid, and I know how atrocity begins. I did not put everything I learned in that file. My subordinate put that in about Donovan's family. I would have forbidden it if I were there."

"Damn it, Pavlenko." Charlie threw him back on the bed.

The Russian used this latest release to put some distance between himself and Charlie. He scrambled to the end of the bed, pulling his shirt down over the new dressing.

"I am getting to it. Give me time to explain!"

"What's in the file about Mara? Now, Pavlenko. Now!"

Pavlenko stared, stunned. "You are very much like your father."

John put the gauze back in the bag.

"The file is standard," said Pavlenko. "It has not much more than in Frank's file. Much of what's in it came from Frank's file. His office is riddled with moles, though he has been more careful since the tragedy. I have, too. I do not include everything I know, like...."

"Like?"

"That you are Mara's biological brother. You have different mothers, but the same father. I know this but did not put it in the file."

John stood, scissors in one hand, tape in the other. The patient rose to his feet, back against the wall, trapped. Charlie advanced.

"If it is not in the file, Sergei Nickolaevich, why are you so worried about it?" Charlie took another step closer.

"It is not in the file. I found it here." Sergei pointed to his head. "I am no fool, but I am also not a genius. You are only the second one I have met."

"And the other?"

The Russian shrugged. "Is in my directorate."

"And the file?"

"Contains the verification."

"What the hell are you talking about?" John dropped scissors and tape and stepped forward. "What difference does it make if she's step or biological or from Mars or Pluto? And what verification? Of what?"

Both men looked at him, puzzled. "It makes no difference to us," said Charlie, finally. "But to many of our enemies, genetics are everything. They are obsessed with heredity, race, and eugenics. They will think it is important to us, also. They will think it makes her more critical to us as if that were possible. The daughter and sister of living specialists is an irresistible temptation. We would risk everything."

"You are risking everything," said Sergei.

John looked at Charlie and pointed to his patient. "Your enemies already sent him to kill her. Why is this different? And, by the way, have any of you heard that the Cold War is over? It's been in the news."

"It is not over," said Charlie. "It is only on pause."

"This is merely a rearrangement of terms and alliances," agreed Sergei.

"And the order given to Sergei was casual," said Charlie. "A kind of one-off designed to prevent a future problem, should she become remarkable. But as my father's daughter, and as my sister, she becomes remarkable immediately. She inherits all our enemies as well." He turned to Pavlenko. "What is your verification, Sergei Nickolaevich?"

"First, I will tell you how I thought of it. May I sit down? Shall we all sit down? Will you let me finish without hitting me?"

FIFTEEN

Charlie guaranteed nothing, except that he could make John shudder with a glance. Sergei took the cold stillness as an affirmative and sat in a wing-back chair before a low coffee table. John sat beside him in a matching chair. Charlie took a desk chair and put it on the other side of the table, facing them. Sergei winced and wheezed, shifting in his seat. He would have been more comfortable lying on the bed, but then, comfort was a relative thing in a room with Charlie.

"I told you I was assigned to watch her," said Sergei. "I have also watched you, during the period when we had you in Tbilisi and at other times. Within a month of my surveillance of Mara, I was struck by her resemblance to you. It is not only in looks. Such things are difficult to tell. Vasily Sobieski was Ukrainian and Polish; Alexandra Dolnikova is American, but her parents were Russians. Mara should be one hundred percent Slav, but she is not, just as you are not, despite your Russian mother."

The corners of Charlie's mouth turned down. Sergei winced and hurried to continue.

"This is something that I know and that I realized soon after my assignment began, but it was on the level of a hunch or an intuition that is useless without verification. It is worse than useless if it causes an intelligence officer to read things into a situation that are not there.

"So when I first noticed her coolness, the still walk —a movement, really, not a walk, with no discernible effort expended—that could change from barely perceptible to a blur of speed during the time it takes to blink the eye, I told myself, of course, she would resemble you. No doubt you trained her."

He waited.

"I taught her to shoot," said Charlie. "Louis and I did. Vasily and Steve taught her to fight. That's where the speed comes from."

"Even more reason why it should not remind me of you. No. There is another quality in the way she moves and the way she speaks. Your father has it, too, I notice now, but I have not watched him as much."

"Yes," said John. "I've seen it, too."

Charlie stared at him and he clamped his jaw shut.

"I pushed the idea away for three weeks," said Sergei. "Then, I could not help myself. I reviewed everything I could remember in the file, and that is considerable. I have memorized most of it. Two events in the year before Mara's birth may be significant. About seven and a half months before her birthdate, we know that Charlemagne assassinated a mole in St. Louis. Their jet stopped in Chicago before leaving the country. The next week, Sobieski married Alex Dolnikova in Capri. We have that. We have Mara's date of birth from her American passport. We do not have her birth weight, which should be low after only seven and a half months."

"And the other event?" asked Charlie sharply.

Sergei inhaled deeply. "Six weeks before the assassination in St. Louis, Charlemagne stopped a terrorist team called Ill Wind in the act of trying to blow up the Sears Tower in Chicago. Have they told you this?"

Charlie gave only his still stare.

"Frank Cardova's reports were usually very detailed, quite excellent. All his reports were excellent."

"Don't flatter him to his face that way, or he will rob me of my chance to kill you, Sergei."

"I am touched by your concern." Sergei placed his hand over his heart.

"Frank's report contained much juicy detail," he continued, "including the fact that Alex played a role in the operation, but nothing about what that role was, other than that she was hurt in some way, largely unimportant, though not to her, I am sure. What is conspicuous is what is missing, like her name and a description of what she wore that night. Frank does not miss much, and he did not miss this, either, and commented on not being able to discover it. This means he was not there for much of the time during the hours preceding the operation and had no say in the use and possible abuse of a bystander."

"I don't want to hear your babysitter backbiting, Pavlenko. Get to the verification. Is it in Frank's report? If so, his office has it, too, and if it's as riddled as you say...."

"No. It is not in his report. It is in something only we have, and only by accident. We have a torn, yellow copy of a copy of an old Bulgarian interrogation report, a tedious, very detailed report. We have it only because the subject is Sobieski. I do not think anyone except me ever read it, at least not through and through. I read it long ago when I was still young and enthusiastic, but I still have some of it, here." He pointed to his head. "This is what I went back to Moscow to check, to verify, and that is how I knew about Semianov's copy."

"Get to it." Just like that. Flat, expressionless. Charlie stood when he said it, stepped behind his chair, one hand on the chair, one in a pocket. Even the movement seemed motionless, a mere rumor, he was so still when it ended.

"Sobieski was twenty-two when the Bulgarians had him. One of the tortures they used, while it would not castrate him, could certainly sterilize. Probably did."

"That's it?"

"He said nothing, by the way, for all their efforts."

"Probably sterilize?"

"Well, add to that the record of offspring—you must know they were a wild bunch in their younger days, The Frenchman left half a dozen bastards around the world that he does not know about."

"And my father?"

"He was more selective. There are two possibilities, but the women were well-connected and had other men to claim paternity."

"But Vasily?"

"None. He married almost ten years after that interrogation. Six weeks before the marriage, a confused muddle of an operation involving the bride. Interesting."

"Why didn't you tell my father about this?"

"How? How do I begin? Do I say, 'Mara is your daughter and I can verify it?' Does he know it already, or would I be the first to tell him? Do I want to be the first to tell him? I did the prudent thing. I shut up. Always the wisest policy when the wrong word will kill you."

Charlie smiled slightly. "He found out only a few days ago."

"How did he react? Did he kill the messenger?"

Charlie shook his head. "Alex told him. He was the last to know. Mara was always important; she could not help but be, but now? It is his little Nadia restored, though Mara is nothing like her. Nadia was untouched by life. There was no blemish allowed near her. I thought even toadstools would march away at the sound of her footsteps in a forest. Nothing rotten could withstand her approach."

He sat again, looking downward and into the past. "Nadia was like my mother. Mara is more like me and my father. I do not mean to say she kills. She does not. I mean that she lives more completely on earth and less in heaven. My mother never accepted what my father does. She did not disagree with it or dispute about it; she ignored it. It did not exist for her. Nadia was the same."

Charlie stood a second time, both hands in his pockets, head tilted. John wondered at the stillness with which the man mastered his emotion

"When I was seventeen," he continued. "I took them both, and Mara, too, to the television room. A news program showed pictures from Thailand, where a bus full of people had been held hostage by terrorists. They showed the bus burning and the rescued people and their families, crying. I said, 'See Mama, Papa rescued these people, he and Vasily and Louis, and they will be home in two hours. Louis has been badly burned. We must be ready to help them.' My mother smiled at me. 'Nonsense,' she said. 'Listen to the television. The Thai government arranged the rescue. What imagination you have!'"

The patient shifted in his chair glancing warily from John to Charlie. John held his breath. The air, the words felt... dangerous.

"Only Mara was there with me when they came in," said Charlie. "My mother told friends that Louis had pneumonia. Mara helped to dress Louis's burned legs. Every few hours she would wet down the dressing. She held his hand while he cried. She was seven."

They could hear Pavlenko's wheeze in the silence. Then Charlie said, "The other genius in your directorate, is it Maximovich?"

Sergei squirmed but did not answer. Charlie turned and left the room.

"The Frenchman's magic box is there on the chest, Doctor." Sergei stumbled to the bed and fell onto it, letting his head rest on the first aid kit. "Quickly, please."

"You need to start doing without the drugs now. I can get you some aspirin."

Pavlenko's answer was in Russian. John understood the meaning without knowing the words.

"Listen, Doctor, I am in pain," Sergei said in English. "I want to sleep. I must sleep. Any addiction you give me will last only until I am shot in a few days."

"How can you talk like that?"

"I know it is wishful thinking. But I fear Mack's knife; I fear it more than a bullet. He used the knife on my specialist, you know, the one who killed Sobieski. I saw the photos."

"Surely, you don't think...."

"I don't think Charlie would tell such things to a living man. Which calls into question your status, Doctor." His voice trailed off as John injected the blessed poison.

SIXTEEN

Seal heard "Oomph," as he opened the bedroom door. Frank was right again.

It started with Charlie and Mara arguing in the dining room. Mack played referee. They used lingo Seal didn't know, but Frank soaked it up. You could see the man was in intelligence heaven, learning bits and pieces that he could never write down and so what use was it, anyway? Jay was still downstairs in the RV, and the Russian was awake and lounging around against the wall with his hands in his pockets. While the battle raged, Donovan slipped off down the hall and the Frenchman followed him. Frank looked at Seal and tilted his head toward the hallway. 'Doctor,' he mouthed silently.

Protect the doctor. The doctor still slept in the room where Pavlenko and Charlie had stowed him earlier. The man could sleep, for sure. Must be part of doctor training. Seal's first glimpse into the gloomy room confirmed the "Oomph." Doc was up against the wall, held there by Donovan, whose fist forced another "Oomph" out of him. The Frenchman stood by like another buzzard waiting for dinner. The two buzzards turned when Seal walked into the room. He stood ten feet from them. Donovan turned back to the doctor, who was still trying to breathe. "Go away," he said over his shoulder.

"No."

There was a pause. "Listen, Seal, this is none of your business." Donovan still did not turn around.

Seal sweated, wiped his forehead with the back of his hand, sweated some more. "I ain't leaving. Mack approved me staying on as a babysitter. Frank told me to talk to the doctor. I'm here to talk to the doctor. That's my story and I'm stickin' to it."

What a stupid time to try to be funny. Seal had this lame theory about a good laugh being just the thing to defuse a touchy situation.

The Frenchman frowned at him. Donovan punched the doc in the gut again.

Jokes are no good with people who don't know the whole language.

"Steve." That's all the Frenchman said, just "Steve," and he let go and the doctor slumped to the floor, a little bit blue. The two specialists walked out of the room then, leaving Seal to his private triumph, because that's what it was, simple, spectacular, victory. He could look Frank in the eye, not as an equal, maybe, but not as a loser babysitter, either. The doc was safe, and it was because of him. For now. He was safe for now.

Seal helped him stand up. He brought him over to a chair and put him in it. The doc's color came back, kind of blotchy in places, but he wasn't blue anymore and you could hear him breathing now.

"I... don't understand. Why...?"

"Just breathe, Doc. We'll talk in a minute." Seal sat in the chair across from him. "You okay, Doc?"

The doctor nodded. "Why? It's not like I'm getting anywhere with her, is it? I can't get close to her, haven't spoken with her all day long. What the hell is Donovan's problem?"

"Ah. In identifying the problem, Doc, I mean in defining, in general, whose it is, you might want to own up to it, seeing as how it's you gettin' beat up all the time. Just a suggestion."

The doctor stared at him. Seal noticed that the doc's eyes were almost as blue as Mack's, and almost as hard as Charlie's. But these eyes didn't make him shake.

"I don't get it," said the doctor. "How is it my problem? I have nothing against him. He's the aggressor."

Seal chuckled. "That's okay then. You didn't do nothing to deserve it, so that means Steve didn't really hit you, so you guys are in conflict resolution or something except that Steve's not totally resolved. That's all."

"But I didn't. I did not provoke this, even if you take Mara into account."

"I don't think Mara has that much to do with it. Maybe at first, but not now, and you don't have to provoke it for it to be real, do you Doc? That last punch sounded pretty real to me. The hate that goes with it was, too, and it don't matter what your intentions are. Steve hates you and that's that."

"Why? It's not rational!"

"Of course not. These guys are more and more not rational as the hours go by, Doc. You're like a sliver stuck under their fingernail. Everything about you is right and good and safe and confident, and none of that applies to them and they hate you for it. You're a foreign body. They're like white whadda yacallits, corpuscles. You bother them."

The doctor wrinkled his brow.

"You ain't afraid, Doc. You ain't and you should be. To them, that means you're stupid or you're privileged or you're dirty and have somethin' up your sleeve. You oughtta shake a little like I do. They don't usually bother babysitters. We're beneath their notice."

"Why should I be afraid? And why on earth would I give Donovan the satisfaction of showing it?"

Seal left his mouth open for a minute before he could answer this doozy. "Somebody's going to die in the next couple days, Doc. This ain't the evening news. It ain't gonna cut to a slick deodorant commercial and come out smelling nice."

"Mack used the TV metaphor, too."

"'Cause it applies. Lots of people who watch TV— and I'm a great channel surfer, don't get me wrong— they think everything's gonna be all right in the end. You do, Doc. You came in here with no experience, watched a man get beat up, sewed him up, got hit yourself a couple times, listened to the commissioning of a murder, and didn't even have the sense to tremble when a guy with a gun let you know he didn't have no use for you at all. You think you're gonna live through it, maybe because you're such a great surgeon. But truth is, even great surgeons die young. The world ain't nice and these guys ain't nice and the people hunting them ain't even nicer. Death stinks, and it's permanent. We're all scared shitless, and you walk around worrying about gettin' close to a girl. You're out of sync."

John's brow wrinkled as he leaned forward. "What can I do? Let's say I own the problem; what the hell is the solution?"

Seal shrugged. He rubbed his nose with a fat, crooked forefinger. "I don't think there's anything you can do. Now climb down there, Doc. I know the look an' I ain't taking it from you. You roll your eyes like you're my better, by money, looks, and education, and I risked my neck just now to save yours, so get off it. That's one thing about Mara. She is superior to me in a lot of ways, but she never, ever let on. Always acted like I was the boss, respected me, even when she was doing what the hell she pleased."

"I thought you were her boss."

"As far as that's possible, on paper, with Mara. That's another subject. Right now, we babysitters are getting tired of worrying about you. Trouble is, there ain't a lot you can do about other people's hate, once it starts. Some hate you because you're like them, others hate you 'cause you're different. Once the hate starts, though, you can change a hundred-eighty and it won't stop. Any change you try to make is hated, too. And that's if change is possible, which in your case I don't think it is. It just ain't in your nature to act like your world shouldn't spill over into everybody else's.

"So you could try avoiding Steve, but that's gonna get real hard when we all move into that RV. Quarters is tight, as they say. You could defend yourself so that it's a draw and then you guys just bare your teeth at each other. I don't see you getting good enough to beat Donovan in five years, though, let alone in five minutes, which it's gonna have to be. Seal rubbed a knuckle on the side of his nose, thinking. "How about gettin' yourself an ally?"

"An ally?"

"Yeah. Somebody who could fight Donovan to a draw, and better yet, who wouldn't have to. Somebody he respects, to be kind of on your side."

John shook his head. "Mack said he wouldn't protect me."

"I don't know nothing about that, Doc."

"What about Charlie?"

Seal shook his head, rubbed his nose again, and scratched behind an ear. "Charlie's got his hands full with Mara. Not a good one to approach. And somehow, I don't see you seeking help from Mara, either, am I right?"

John nodded.

"That leaves the Frenchman."

John pointed to his eye.

"Doc, that's perfect. It gives you an opening. I mean, it'd be tough to walk up to him and say 'How 'bout helping me stay alive?' Thanks to that shiner, all you have to do is apologize. He'll figure it out and he'll have to be on your side, more or less."

John gripped the arms of the chair. "Apologize for what? He hit me!"

"For calling him a liar."

"He is a liar."

"No, he ain't." Seal tried one of those looks full of meaning but the doctor was not translating.

"He lied to me!"

"No, he didn't." Seal did not hide his exasperation. "It was a joke, a game. Don't you see that? Didn't
all those college classes teach you anything?"

"A joke! He said there were no drugs for pain!"

"He didn't expect you to believe it, Doc. Didn't
you see it in his eyes? You know a lot about bodies,
but you don't know nothin' about people. People are
more than bodies. The Frenchman said there ain't any
drugs because he meant he wanted the Russian to suffer, but people don't like saying that kind of thing out
loud. He said it with his eyes, and you just listened to
the words."

"Oh." Pause. "Tell me what to do." He held out his
hands, a supplicant.

"Draw him aside and tell him you're sorry you
said that. You were wrong. That's all. He'll know what
you're getting at. He might call the snarling dog off
you."

John stood up and turned toward the door.

"Wait," said Seal, also standing. "You can't go to
him looking pitiful. You need to clean up. Charlie said
he left some clean clothes out for you." He looked
around the room. "Here they are." He picked up a
small pile of clothes from the bed, the green polo shirt
on top, and handed it to the doctor. "There's a shower
in there." He pointed to a small en-suite bathroom.
"There's a razor in there, too. You'd better shave 'cause
we're all going downstairs tonight."

"Why?"

"It's decided that we'll explain your being here as Mara's boyfriend. So you two have to go downstairs and act like a number. Charlie and Steve will go with us. I'll be your babysitter. We'll probably meet the Jared dame and the lawyer and her FBI toad. We hope so. Our job is to keep them busy while Mack, Louis, and Frank sneak the Russian into the RV."

John shifted his weight from foot to foot. "Seal," he said doubtfully.

"Yeah, Doc?"

"Why is the FBI on both sides of this? I thought—when Jay came for me, I understood—I was working for the FBI. Who, exactly, is who around here?"

Seal held up both hands. "Don't ask me. I'm just an old counterintelligence officer turned babysitter. I only know I belong on Mara's side. Jay Turner wants that list Pavlenko says he's got. He wants it bad. So do a lot of people, including this lawyer we'll see downstairs. Frank wants information and he wants to prevent a disaster, God help him. Pavlenko wants to stay alive. Mara wants to be in charge. I don't know what the rest are up to, but I don't think they give a shit about the list. They'd like to kill Pavlenko, I know. There's some bad blood there for sure. They're concerned about Mara, big time, and as far as that goes, I guess I'm an ally of sorts. What about you, Doc?"

"Do you think Mara's in danger?"

"You bet. This game ain't Trivial Pursuit. Word is, wear body armor if you got any. Get washed, Doc. We got twenty minutes."

SEVENTEEN

"Where's that fuckwad doctor?" asked Steve. "Talking to Louis," said Charlie.

Seal stood with the others in the anteroom before the elevator, all of them looking washed and pressed though fatigue created circles around their eyes. Steve's exhaustion took the form of a restless irritability. Seal yawned. Charlie was as still as ever, Mack more so. Jay had his hands in his pockets, his lips pursed in a silent whistle. Pavlenko came through the double doors dressed in a black sweatsuit. Frank toddled in after him. Finally, Louis and the doctor joined the crowd in the small room. Footsteps were loud on the tile floor. Louis mumbled something to Steve. They all waited for Mara.

She sure could do an entrance. Seal tore his eyes off her long enough to look around quickly. Mack's eyes were concentrated on the skirt. Yes, Seal admitted silently, it was pretty short. Real short. There were only about four inches of shiny purple fabric beneath the glittery soft sweater that hung below the hips and covered the gun. The rest was leg, all the way to the high heels. He glanced around again. Mara cleared her throat, and finally, a few eyes moved to her face. She had her hair up and twisted in the back. Her earrings must have been zircons. They dangled a little and sparkled like her sweater when she moved.

Seal could see that Mack disapproved, deeply, but nobody else did. Jay let his heavy jaw stay open. The rest managed to disguise their delight, though they still concentrated on those magnificent legs.

"Sir, this is appropriate dress for an American woman of my age." She said it firmly but without defiance.

"What sort of American woman?" said Mack.

Louis smiled. "Americans are not concerned with such distinctions. The woman I had last night was quite indistinguishable from a party of wealthy banker's wives in the piano lounge."

Mack frowned at him. "Are you saying American harlots look like respectable women, or that respectable American women look like harlots?"

Louis grinned. "You are turning red, Misha. I am saying that, in this culture, Mara looks respectable, not otherwise. The presence of Charlie, Steve, and the doctor will prevent any unwanted signals, and I think the outfit is perfect. Anything less would make her look out of place. Besides, it is simple charity to give the watchers something decent to look at. Their eyes will be glued to her, and we will have no trouble getting our KGB friend into the vehicle without being seen. Stop wanting to shoot everybody for enjoying what you never failed to enjoy in the past."

Mack looked doubtful, glanced again at Louis, glared at the doctor who was enjoying himself too obviously, and sighed. "You had better go," he said to Charlie.

Mara's smile broke out in full force in the elevator until Charlie turned it off with a warning scowl. He turned back to face the door and Mara stuck her tongue out at him. "I saw that," he said, though he could not possibly have.

The evening began in the piano bar where they found Jane, Roger, and Judy, ordered scotch all around (to keep it simple, said Charlie), and sat looking at the silent piano. Seal gagged on the scotch and wished for a beer. Charlie yielded to pressure and played the Litolff Scherzo at the doctor's request. Mara watched Jane carefully. Seal watched them all.

There was no doubt the Jared woman was beautiful. But while Mara's beauty was something you had to be careful not to break, Jane's was the kind that would break you. She was tall, even taller than Charlie and all of it leg. She also wore her skirt short, so that in a leg-to-leg competition, Seal reluctantly named her the winner over Mara. There could be no contest in the rest of their beauty, though, because they were too different to be compared to each other. They were exquisite examples of their types; any choice would be in the chooser. Jane's voluminous brown hair could not be tamed by a French twist like Mara's. Her honey-colored skin was flawless; her long, perfect nose balanced a long, perfect face in which her eyes, as brown and large as Steve's, held no hint of softness. This woman was only for the adventurous type. Seal suppressed a shudder, acknowledging to himself that he was never all that adventurous.

The lawyer was something else again. She was not ugly. Under good management, she could probably hold her own in the company of any woman on a rung just below Jane and Mara. The problem was, there was no management at all. Judy Simons had her hair done at the Bad Haircut Emporium. Clothes by Show The Lumps. Makeup under the direction of Blotch and Disfigure. Worst of all was the way this specimen clung to Steve Donovan like plastic wrap.

Wasn't he the funniest, the handsomest person? She simpered until the giggles ran up and down Seal's spine like fingernails on a blackboard.

Not man, 'person' was the word she used when she talked about Steve. In five minutes of giggling inanity, Seal decided the woman had no concept of the masculine and was not even aware that this was the quality that attracted her. While Steve was good looking, maybe, he wasn't the best looking of the bunch. That had to go to Charlie. But Steve was the most thoroughly, instinctively male 'person' Seal had ever met. Yep. He carried a lot of his personality in his gonads. He was funny, too, quick witted, slow speaking, with just a hint of his native Texas drawl. Sometimes his humor was cruel. It was always aggressive.

A crowd formed around the piano. Roger and Seal exchanged concerned glances. Charlie finished the Scherzo and accepted the applause with a solemn, stiff bow. Roger ushered them all out, with Charlie none too pleased, until Seal showed him the bottle of single malt he had procured, and they went upstairs to Roger's room to drink it.

Roger had your basic single room with a connecting door to Judy's basic single room. They managed to get two chairs out of Judy's room before she yanked Steve through the connecting door, saying "It's our turn," and locked it behind them. This left the rest of them to find a place in Roger's room for the important business of drinking Charlie's scotch together and watching each other for mistakes.

They gathered at the far end of the room from the entrance door. To the right of that door was the connection to the other room. From there to the chair where Jane sat, a hotel dresser stretched along the right-hand wall, holding Roger's suitcase, an ice bucket, assorted hotel pamphlets, an ashtray, and a television.

Jane and Charlie held court in chairs between the dresser and the far wall. Nearest to them stood a small, round table, leaned on by Roger who sat in the chair beside it. Seal sat at the other side of the table.

The bed was centered on the left wall of the room. Here, Mara leaned against the headboard and stretched her lovely legs before her, demurely crossed at the ankle. John sat on the bed next to her, close to the edge.

The match began and the trouble started right away.

"How long have you known Mara?" Jane asked the doctor.

"Not long," John said simply. He was as cool as anybody could want. No sweat.

"What happened to your eye, Doctor?"

"Please, call me John." He paused, sizing her up, as one Frigidaire to another. "I ran into a fist." He smiled as if the joke were original.

"Over a girl?" There was a dimple in Jane's smile, more mischievous than endearing.

"What else is there to fight about?"

Old MacArthur's speech ran through Seal's mind. Duty. Honor. Country.

The conversation, if it could be called that, kept going this way for a few minutes.

Seal and Roger watched the exchange between Jane and the doctor like spectators at a tennis match. It was a civilized game until it became a doubles tourney with Mara's first volley.

"You've known Charlie a long time, haven't you Jane?"

"We met ten years ago if that's what you mean."

"That was when he saved your life, wasn't it?"

Charlie gave Mara an obvious shut-up signal.

She ignored it. "Wasn't it Charlie who shot some guy trying to kill you? What was he called? The Barracuda, wasn't it? Charlie nailed him and saved your life, as I recall."

The shut-up signal became insistent. Nope, thought Seal as he watched the Jared girl's big brown eyes, sorry Mara. Jared has no remorse. Nothing will soften that resolve. You're right. She's here to kill him.

"Since you weren't there, Mara, you must be an avid reader," said Jane.

Ah. There's a reaction from Charlie. At least he has to acknowledge that she's in the game. She knows about files, and she knows about research. Point, Mara.

"I remember little of it, myself," continued the Jared woman, "except an unfortunately vivid recollection of your father cutting a man's throat."

Ace.

Charlie changed the signal. Seal did not understand it, though it seemed to be directed at him. No, not at him, past him. The doctor. Of course. The doctor gathered Mara in his arms and dutifully kissed her.

Your father... your father.... It might have been a fruitful reflection, but it was driven out of Seal's head by Steve and Judy's entrance. The doctor sat up at the edge of the bed. Mara smoothed herself and sat next to him. Steve pushed Seal out of his chair and sat in it, within arm's reach of John. Seal made the air conditioner at the window groan under his weight. Roger gave his chair to Judy, who moved it closer to Steve and took his left hand. Roger sat on the dresser next to the TV. Single malt made the rounds again and everybody had a fill-up.

This was appalling and Seal found himself thinking about how sane and unambiguous a James Bond movie was, with all the women beautiful and understanding. Not ridiculous and demanding like this lawyer. Bond's women weren't carved out of tombstone granite like Jared, nor were they dangerously intelligent like Mara. Oh, for the good old days of espionage. At least then, you knew who your enemies were. They were the ones who fed you to the sharks. This was Seal's second glass of scotch and he wasn't used to it. He caught himself seeing sharks.

The lawyer was babbling something about fancy Eastern schools only letting in quota blacks, which earned her daggers from Jared and made her backpedal frantically to correct the mistake, because Jane was black, an obvious thing that was easy to overlook and made Seal almost feel sorry for the lawyer. When you saw Jane for the first time you might say to yourself "Wow, what a stunner!" or "I don't wanna mess with that iceberg," but never, "By golly, she's black."

One more discomfort endured. How many more to go?

Judy let go of Steve's hand and reached over him to squeeze the doctor's knee. "You really shouldn't turn so many shades of red over a little kissy face, John. We're all adults here, except maybe for Mara. But then, in her case, it's experience over age that matters most."

Seal sucked in his lips, tried to suck them right down his throat. The woman's got a death wish, he thought. The shut-up signal was flying through the room, ignored. Would Mara understand the lawyer? Was her English good enough for this? There was a lot of vocabulary she was missing, Seal knew, and he hoped there was still a big gap in the sexual insult domain. He watched her, same as everybody else.

She was so still. Her face became a perfect, pleasant blank. She smiled a little.

Oh God, she got it.

"I'm trying to remember," she said sweetly, "the term for someone with plenty of age, but no experience. Old maid, isn't it?" She cocked her head at Seal and raised an eyebrow.

He kept his lips sucked into his cheek and tried his own version of Shut Up.

Mara ignored his signal, too. "Typical of an important broad like yourself, though, Judy. With no tits and no man."

"You bitch," was Judy's frank reply. "It's only fair to warn you that I'm armed." She reached under her blouse and pulled out an enormous .357 revolver with a six-inch barrel, thus explaining and eliminating one lump. She began waving the thing around.

Charlie, Jane, Steve, Roger, and Seal all had their hands on their weapons but did not draw them yet because, so far, the lawyer couldn't get her finger in the trigger guard. Mara was perfectly still and did not reach for her Glock. She waited.

To Judy she said, "I see you have your very own," she looked at Seal, who was not about to help even if he knew the direction her words were going, "... dick. So why do you want to pull on Steve's?"

The finger found the trigger and the barrel swiveled toward Mara with the sound of a female snarl, but the hammer was never cocked because in the next moment, the revolver flew across the room and the lawyer landed on the floor with a whoosh of expelled air and a thud. The chair she vacated fell against the window and tipped over. It, too, made a thud, the last sound made until she caught her wind and began to shriek, "I'll sue you, Bitch!" between wet sobs. By now everybody was standing; only Mara was smiling, and Seal noticed the doctor shudder right along with him. At Charlie's direction, Doc and Steve helped the bleeding woman to her room. The physical damage was not excessive: a fat lip, a loose tooth, and a bloody nose, but the shrieking did not let up. Words could not express how sorry they were for Roger as they left him, so they didn't use any. Seal shook his hand with a sympathetic look. Condolences. Jane refused an escort to her room, and anyway, they didn't know where that was, and she wasn't about to tell them. She left them by the stairs.

They rode the elevator up to the penthouse in excruciating silence.

EIGHTEEN

Mara lost a high-heeled shoe in the elevator room as she fought Charlie on their way to the dining room. The other shoe came off when she tripped over the two steps into the sunken living room. Charlie had her firmly by the arm, though, so she did not fall on her face.

"That hurts. Stop twisting!" She did her best, her very best, to sound defiant. Tears will ruin my make-up, she told herself, but she could not stop the flood. It did hurt, the way he held her arm. It was also embarrassing to be dragged through the living room and hallway with stocking feet and running mascara.

She discarded defiance in the dining room and replaced it with fear. She had thought she did, but really, she did not know this man. Yes, she had grown up with the body. She recognized the blond, blue-eyed physical shell she played duets with on Christmas mornings. But the man who held her against the wall was not Michael; he was somebody named Charlie, somebody nasty and hard and incredibly angry with her.

Mara grew up surrounded by violent men but never saw this much violence in the eyes of any of them. She was an expert shot and an expert fighter and she was utterly helpless against the fury that held her. He was stronger. He was more determined.

She was afraid.

She allowed the fear to register on her face because she had no choice. She could not disguise it.

He spoke in a low voice, in German, through his teeth. "You will kill us all if you do not learn obedience. When I give you a signal, you are to obey instantly. Less than that is death. Before I let you kill us, I will tie you up without mercy and glue your nose in a corner for the duration of your time here. This is not a threat. Is my first point clear to you?"

She nodded. Her chin hit the top of his hand.

His eyes still burned holes through her.

"Point two," he said. "You will apologize to Steve for referring to him in that disrespectful way. Again, clear?"

Another nod.

"Finally, you will stop provoking the men here. Don't try to look ignorant. You are deliberately provoking them, especially Steve, by the way you speak and the things you wear. No more short skirts; no more gutter language."

She was genuinely confused. "Gutter?"

"Words like broad, dick, and tit are improper."

"They are the words Seal uses."

"Seal is a peasant, for the love of God!"

"He has been very good to me."

"That does not change his class nor require you to change yours. When you speak that way, especially as a woman, you lower yourself. You make yourself an object of pursuit. You become available. Not only the words you use, but the subjects they describe are improper for you to address. You are not a man. You cannot be a man. When you speak that way you do not erase this fact, you emphasize it. I want your word that there will be no more short skirts and no more inappropriate language."

She hung her head. Her tears fell on his hand. She remembered the language used by Louis's beloved wife and quashed her doubts so they would not be visible to Michael. He would only call Millie a peasant, too.

"Tears will not stop me. I will have your word, or you will suffer."

She looked up at him, exasperated and shielding a rebellion. "I can't! I don't understand you. First, I am told I cannot wear jeans. Now, I am told no skirts. All of my skirts are short. What am I to wear? Mama never covered the English words for some things. I have only Seal's words. How do I know what is appropriate? Am I limited to dinner table topics? The weather and general health? Should I blush when men say things, or won't that make them even more uncomfortable?"

His grip loosened, then he let go, and she realized she'd been standing on her toes. His jaw worked, but he said nothing. He still breathed like a maddened bull. "You will obey me," he said finally.

He was dropping the subject, the uncomfortable, excruciating subject. Mara felt new tears—of joy. "Oh yes, yes. I give you my word. And I will apologize to Steve. I promise."

She promised but was not ready to fulfill it in the very next instant when Michael yanked the door open and stomped out of the room. Steve had been sitting by the door, discouraging intruders. He slipped into the room as Michael left it and closed the door quietly behind him.

Ready or not, she had to make the effort. "I... I'm... I apologize for being... for saying..." The tears would not stop.

He wiped a few drops from her cheek, gently. She could see the kiss coming. She was still standing with her back against the corner wall where Michael had put her. There was no graceful exit.

Sergei's kiss had been momentary, and the swelling on his face made him gentle. John had been acutely aware of both Steve and Charlie when he kissed her in Judy's room. His was a longer kiss than Sergei's, and more insistent, but by necessity, chaste.

Steve was under no restraint.

He engulfed her. Her eyes were wide open; he looked at her briefly and forced her mouth open with his tongue. She put her hands on his shoulders to push him away. One of his hands—he must have twenty—went under her sweater and up her back. It slipped under her bra strap and around to the front, where it cupped her breast while his tongue drove deeper into her mouth. She stopped pushing at his shoulders and tried removing that hand. Another of his twenty hands was behind her, lifting her skirt and driving between her legs. Her body began to respond. It was an utterly new sensation to her, an importunate warmth that made her press against him almost involuntarily. He knew it immediately and pressed himself into her as his hand found the top elastic of her panties.

She was terrified, even before the door opened. When it opened, she thought of new reasons for terror, each one more logically deadly than the last. She understood a lot now. She wanted to run and tell Michael that she would give her word to anything he said. She prayed to God that this was not Michael at the door. She wondered why the intruder did not affect Steve. Surely he knew the door was open. He knew it and was beyond caring.

The door opener cleared his throat.

Steve disengaged the kiss. He rested his cheek against hers. His hands stopped moving, but they did not leave the premises. He sighed lightly.

"What, Frank?"

Frank cleared his throat again. "I thought you might need to know, Mack is looking for you."

Steve let her go. He looked at her before he turned around. In one glance, he told her he was determined and expected to succeed.

He put his hand on Frank's shoulder on his way out. "You're a pal, Frank. A real pal."

"Just doing my job, Steve," Frank said quietly.

Mara stood looking stupidly at Frank. Her skirt was hiked up around her waist. She smoothed it down, turning crimson. She could feel the tears beginning again. Frank had interviewed her once when he recruited her into the game. That was the only time before now that she had met him. Her confusion was total. He was male and he was a stranger and she feared him. Yet, Misha trusted him, somewhat. Thank God it was not Misha who found Steve kissing her like that.

"Can I help you in any way, Miss Sobieski?"

He didn't move. That was good. That helped. She had time to edge away from the wall, to prepare a defense, which she worked on until she realized the absurdity. Frank was not Steve. He was no match for her.

"Do you know...?" Her voice squeaked. She brought it under control but could not stop her legs from trembling. "Do you know where Louis is?"

"He's on the terrace. Would you like me to take you to him?" He held out his arm to her like a dinner partner.

It was the return of civilization, a reinstatement of safety that stopped the earth quaking under her feet. She rested her hand lightly on his arm and let him lead her to the terrace.

Louis leaned on the wall, looking at the neon lights below, his dark head silhouetted by the light from a three-quarter moon above. He turned and left the drink he had in his hand on the wall when he heard Mara running toward him so that his arms were free to embrace her as she buried her face in his chest, sobbing.

NINETEEN

She wailed into Louis's shoulder as he held her. He offered a handkerchief when she surfaced for air. She cried again into the handkerchief.

When the flood subsided, Louis said, "Your big brother has been nasty to you, I suspect."

She nodded.

"And worse than that," said Louis. "He was right, was he not?"

Through the new round of sobs came a few chopped words, "But... I ... proved... Jane's... dirty."

"You are crying over a victory?"

She became calmer now. She blew her nose on the handkerchief, making it a dainty act.

"Why the tears, my little precious one?" Louis held her shoulders and stood back a step to look at her. "What else happened?"

"I don't know. I am confused. This morning I had never been kissed by a man, and now I have been kissed by three and I don't know what to do. You are an expert in these things, Louis. What should I do?"

"I know about Sergei's demonstration," he said, "and I am sure the doctor kissed you while you were downstairs infuriating your brother. Who is the third?"

She hung her head. "I am frightened."

He pursed his lips and nodded. "In one day, you have been kissed by Love, by Infatuation, and by Desire and have discovered that Desire is dangerous."

"Will he... do you think he would rape me?"

"Ah. There is a misapplied word. Steve will not deliberately hurt you to cause you pain. He will overwhelm you and convince himself that you are willing. The word for it was once seduction. Equally damaging at times, but not the same. He will certainly seduce you if you allow it."

"But Misha would kill him. He must know that."

"He does. But Michael is the one who would kill him, *Cheri*. Misha and I had a lifetime of friendship behind us when we had our trouble. Steve and Michael have only ten years. It will not be enough."

Louis took his glass off the wall and refilled it at the little bar near the piano room window. He filled another glass and handed it to Mara. She sipped it and rubbed one ankle with the other foot, trying to work out how best to phrase her question.

"Louis?"

"Yes, *Cheri*."

"The trouble you and Misha had, did it have to do with my mother?"

"Yes."

There are limits to some questions. She was dying to know all of it, every detail, and yet she hated the thought of knowing any of it. In Mara's universe, Louis did no wrong. Her mother on the other hand....

"Why is Steve like this? He never was before."

"You were not fully grown up before. Understand, he is a warrior." Louis leaned on the terrace wall and looked out on the lighted streets below them. "He wants to make you his prize, to conquer you, to collect you the way he collected his new Beretta, to cosset you and keep you, the way he modified the Beretta and cleans it and oils it. You are to be had for your beauty. It is quite simple. If sex were not strongly interesting, we would soon be extinct. If Steve did not behave as a warrior, he would not be on the team."

Mara studied him as he drank. The ice clinked when he put the glass down. The shadows played with his face so that she could not be sure of his expression. He was grim; she could feel it. She tried to imagine him behaving the way Steve had done. Yes, of course. She had always seen the resemblance between these two and wondered what it was. Now she saw it clearly.

"What should my mother have done?"

She meant to say, "What should I do?" She did not often speak her thoughts, and this was the one person to whom she always spoke freely, but would he answer it?

He smiled at her, but not in a jolly way. It was an ironic, regretful smile. "She should have chosen me," he said. "She had three chances to choose me. She trusted luck the first time, and I lost, but I wonder if you would have been so beautiful if it were I and not Misha who drew the ace of diamonds." He touched her cheek as he said this. "She married Vasily. This, also, did not pose a problem to me. But when she chose Misha...." He dropped his arm to his side, drew in a deep breath, and let it out again, slowly. Then he turned away from her, back to the lights of the city.

"That does not help you, I know. Steve is not for you. You cannot choose him. He wants your beauty. Though you grew up near him, though he trained you himself, he knows nothing else about you. The doctor, now, sees you more clearly. He knows that you have a personality and that it is not the same insipid assembly line American girl personality he is accustomed to. He is attracted, but he knows nothing about your training, your strengths, or your weaknesses."

Mara slipped her hand under his arm and leaned with him over the city. "You're saying that Sergei loves me?"

"He does."

"But he never looks at me."

"He carefully never looks at you. He knows Misha will read him at a glance. But all his care is for nothing. Misha knows it already. That is why Sergei is still alive. We know that it is danger to you that made him act, not this list."

"How do you know?"

Louis turned and smiled at her in the moonlight. "Sergei is non-ideological, in many ways like Steve. Ask Steve what he thinks of a socialist, capitalist, or fascist, and he will tell you how to kill one. Sergei is the same. He is loyal to his friends and his job and will do it superbly well without ever thinking or caring about the philosophy that underlies it. Now he is betraying not his country, which does not suffer much by the release of Semianov's outdated list, nor his defunct ideology, but his best friend, Maximovich. It is an enormous betrayal for a man like Sergei. His reason must be compelling. You are the most compelling thing in his life."

"He is trying not to betray him. He is trying not to mention Maximovich," Mara said.

"He is not succeeding. I suspect his friend Volodya is the chief danger."

"Should I choose Sergei?"

"I did not say that. We may yet have to kill him. And even if we do not, Maximovich will not be the only one seeking vengeance."

She searched the lines of streetlights for something to say, quickly, before this line of thought could go on.

"What should I do about Steve?"

"You must be firm with him. Always say no. Never waiver from sentiment or fear. Give him no hope. Never be alone with him. Never be intimate in any way."

"I cannot be friends?"

"No. Business only."

They stood silent, facing each other, for nearly a full minute. Mara sensed a rising urgency in the noises and voices inside, but she did not want to break the spell. There was so much that Louis could explain. She only needed the questions and the time to ask them.

"Jane said she saw my father cut a man's throat," she told him finally.

"Your father?"

"Those were her words. She meant Misha."

"A great victory indeed, little one. Michael cannot deny what she is now. If she knows that, she can only have learned it from Maximovich. But why does it bother you? I sense there is more to it than the obvious discomfort of having Misha as an ancestor. *Blut ist ein ganz besonderer Saft, n'est-ce pas?*"

"Quite so, Mephistopheles."

"You cannot believe Misha could do such a thing, eh?"

"He is so wise and impeccable."

"So, how could he be so unclean?" said Louis. "Soon you will see us all at our filthiest."

"I have seen it," she insisted. "I have cleaned your wounds, washed you, shaved you, and disinfected you. I know it is not pleasant. I am prepared."

"These are physical things. You have not seen the other damage. How can the cold, wise, impeccable Misha perform such a hot crime? The same way we all do. We deny the humanity of the victim and a little of our own dies with him. Should you fear becoming like him? Yes."

"How did you know? Why should I fear it?"

"I know because you would not be here if you were not testing it. You want to know what's inside you. I admire you for not taking the safe road, the squeaky-clean American way to mediocrity and self-delusion, but I am afraid you will not like what you find, my dear."

"What will I find, Louis?" She looked down at her feet. There were holes in the toes of her stockings.

"That, as a killer, you are even worse than Misha, because you are better than he is, not more skilled, but more good. The greatest abomination is killing for goodness' sake. When I kill, I am always evil, careful to be so, a regular Mephistopheles indeed. I am hot with hate and fear, while Misha is cool with plans and procedures. That is why he is in charge, and why Michael is next in charge, and you must obey him, my dear, but that is beside our point for now. You, too, would be a cool killer, one who does the job for some good, but unlike Misha, you are, so far, unaware of the evil. Killing may be justice and it may be necessary, but it is never, ever good, and no matter how good the end, murder is an evil means."

"I do not intend to kill."

"Circumstances will force it, this trip."

"Should I go home? Have I made a mess of things? Have I endangered everyone?"

"Which one first? Yes, you should go home, but we cannot get you there safely. No, you have done what was necessary, and have done well. Yes, you have endangered us all, but not because you had any control over it."

"I wish we could just forget about the stupid list."

"There is also the file."

"And the file."

"There are larger considerations."

"Such as?"

"Jay Turner fears for his precious constitution."

"That does not concern you, Louis. You are not an American."

"True. I am much more concerned with preserving my skin. But Misha dislikes large death tolls if they can be avoided. It is the goodness in him again, and Jay is convinced he must have the list to avert disaster."

Mara sighed and looked at her feet again.

Louis looked at them, too.

"You know that you should not be barefoot in these stockings," he said. "Look. You have big holes in them. Such things can be worn more than once, Mara, if you take care of them."

She chuckled. "You old rogue. You are so cheap."

"Frank called me cheap, too. Last night. He insisted that I tip the woman. You would think that a thousand dollars is sufficient without a tip."

"A thousand dollars! How does she earn it? I am intrigued. What...?"

"Enough education. Come, we must prepare for the drive to San Antonio."

TWENTY

P eople don't build houses, do coronary bypasses or find deadly lists of irrelevant Soviet agents without first holding meetings. Mack convened one as soon as the RV door closed behind John, who was the last person to squeeze in.

"Are you in yet?" Mara asked from somewhere in the crowd.

"Not a question a man likes to hear," said Steve.

Surreptitious chuckles all around, suppressed by a glower from Charlie.

John stood squashed between Steve, who was all elbows, and a small refrigerator that held a computer.

They chose the twenty-seven-foot Jamboree, Seal told him before they climbed inside because there were so many of these on the road.

"But," John protested, "this model was never designed to hold ten people."

"All the better," was Seal's reply. "It'll completely unexpected. And anyway, Jay won't be with us. He'll head for Chicago to try to draw off the lawyer. There will be only nine most of the time."

Nine people in a twenty-seven-foot camper. John did the math. He had seen an ugly mottled green car hitched to the back before he squeezed inside. He wondered if he could ride in that.

"That's for gas," Seal told him. "We put an extra tank in it so we don't have to get the RV wedged into a seedy gas station."

John lingered outside as long as he could. Pavlenko had been squirreled away earlier with Jay Turner to babysit him. The others came on board carrying bags and cases. All of these clanked. The specialists wore black. They wore it unobtrusively: old black denim, black t-shirts, black boots. Mack and Steve wore a top layer of plaid flannel to relieve the uniform look and cover their guns. Mara had already gone in before John got there; he didn't get to see her.

Once inside, he still couldn't see her. He was in the main cabin, no more than two meters from her, but everybody was in the way.

The RV had been modified. On the right, the cabin over the cab was stuffed with what looked like radios, a series of navigation gadgets, and other metal boxes with lighted displays of blinking numbers and dangling phone cords. Beneath the comm bank hung a heavy black curtain that separated the cab from the main cabin. Behind Steve, who stood to his right, the window had also been covered with a black curtain. There were no seats on this side of the cabin, but John could make out Frank's back against the wall as he sat on a footlocker shoved under the little window.

There was a booth of sorts on the other side of the space, with bench seats and a small table attached to the wall under another black-clad window. Mack sat in the corner, and next to him, Charlie. Across from them sat Louis with Mara. John caught a glimpse of her hand on the table. Above the window was a shelf holding a row of television screens showing closed-circuit views of the parking lot around them.

What remained of the galley was to John's left. The small refrigerator served as a computer stand.

Across a narrow aisle, the stove had been removed and replaced with another large, black box, all lights and knobs, topped with a tape apparatus of big and little reels, two each, that turned intermittently by themselves, two at a time, with no apparent human control. Sergei Pavlenko was attached to this machine by a cord running to the headphones he wore. He leaned over the sink, facing the center of the room. To Sergei's left, John caught sight of a restaurant-style coffee maker, and on it, three full, steaming pots. He hoped the cabinet above it held supplies, food being the chief commodity on his mind at the moment.

Seal had wedged himself in the aisle between the sink and the refrigerator to John's left. He smelled suspiciously and unappetizingly of sauerkraut.

The meeting droned on like any other John had ever attended. Speakers spoke at length about things he did not want to understand, like weapons and enemies. He would have fallen over from fatigue, tension, and scotch, but Steve's many elbows caught him every time he nodded.

Jay Turner spoke about the route and the GPS and how that worked. Then came the typical interminable questions, all of which would have been better addressed one-on-one. Nobody asked what the hell GPS meant, which was the one thing John wanted to know but would never dare bring up in this venue, partly because he sensed Steve was just as impatient with the questioners as he was. There would be better opportunities to irritate the man, preferably someplace where there was room to run.

Mack spoke next, packing vital information into every short, accented sentence, forcing John to listen. Most of it did not apply to him, like the admonition not to wear weapons openly in the cab or the restrictions on cleaning your weapon: permitted, because this is not the airplane, but always point to the rear of the vehicle so there is no risk of shooting the driver or the explosives stored above the driver.

John did not miss any of these and other essential points. There would be two watches, one under Mack's direction, the other under Charlie's. The watch up front would drive, monitor the radios, maintain the coffee pot, and take the car to get fuel halfway through the shift. At the end of each four-hour shift, the front watch would go into the back where there were bunks. If your watch was in the back, you could go up front outside your watch time only with permission of the other watch leader. If your watch was in front, you were not permitted to go back until the shift ended. Fighting was prohibited. Why was Mack looking at him? Mack would personally enforce this. John looked at Steve sideways and smiled.

Were there any questions? No. Mack did not inspire questions. The perfect chairman.

He named the watches: Steve and Mara, with Seal as babysitter, on Charlie's watch. The rest were on Mack's. Charlie's watch was up front first. Jay would drive them to the intersection of I-80 and US 95, then he would leave for Chicago, hoping to lure away the lawyer and her FBI helper. Jane Jared, they assumed, would continue to San Antonio by van. She had told Charlie she was attending a political rally there. She had mentioned a van. They had no idea which van, but they had a good touch on Roger's car and were monitoring it with primary and backup tapes.

If Jay's plan worked, and if he succeeded in luring away the lawyer, and if they were able to touch Jared's vehicle, they would devote the machine to her. Otherwise, if they had to monitor both, they would have to split the channels and keep a close eye on the tapes. Assuming they could touch Jared at all, reminded the Frenchman. Assuming so, agreed Mack.

Getting to the back of the RV at the end of the meeting posed another challenge. Jay started the vehicle and was already driving them out of the lot. Seal and Frank did a dance in the middle of the cabin, trying to get past each other without being crushed. Frank, the smaller of the two, had the worse time of it. He pushed John ahead of him through the galley and into the back. John had only enough time to see Pavlenko hand the headphones to Mara.

His pause to look at her backed up traffic in the galley behind him. She wore a black t-shirt, a shoulder holster holding her Glock, black denim pants, black boots, and a large black bow in her hair. Her hair had been severely swept back and pasted to her head with mousse, the length behind taken up in a tight braid and wound into a knot. The bow was attached to the knot. It was a large, black joke, a militantly feminine defiance of that male environment. As John stared at her, Charlie's arm reached out, took the bow, and tossed it into the sink. It landed on a spent coffee filter.

Shoved from behind, John moved through the narrow corridor to the back room. The doors had been removed from the shower on the left and the toilet on the right. A blanket was nailed over the toilet door, the lone concession to Mara. The shower held equipment. John noticed body armor vests stacked on boxes painted in camouflage patterns.

There was no door to the back room. Four cots, of a military sort, were suspended from the walls, two on each side. These were narrow constructions of pipe and olive-green canvas. There were no blankets. Footlockers and bags in olive drab and black ripstop nylon had been piled against the back wall. More of these were stuffed under the lower bunks. John sat on the lower left-hand bunk. Frank nudged his shoulder.

"Come on, Doc," he said. "You're young and in shape. You jump up to the top and let me have this one."

There was nothing to climb. The cots were bolted to the wall, with canvas straps running from their outside edges, fore and aft, also bolted to the wall a few feet above. John vaulted himself into the upper left-hand cot. The ceiling was too low to sit up. He peered over the edge. Frank did not quite fit in his cot. Pavlenko pushed himself up into the cot opposite John. Mack was still up front. The Frenchman opened one of the foot lockers and took out a rifle, then a gun cleaning kit, and swore softly as he rummaged and produced a wad of round cotton cleaning patches. He sat beneath the patient, unloaded the rifle, and began dismantling it.

"Louis," said Sergei.

"Right here," he replied, in French.

"Did you ask him?" Also in French.

"Yes."

"Well?"

"He will consider your request in his decision."

There was a pause.

"What does that mean?"

Louis laughed. He took a cleaning rod and a patch, dipped the patch in solvent, and rammed it through the barrel with a brass rod. "You know better than to tell your fears to your enemy, Sergei Nicko-laevich."

"I thought that since he is an honorable man ..."

"You presume too much on honor."

"It is all I have."

Another pause.

Sergei spoke again: "There is only honor."

"You want my opinion? I am an old killer. In the end, there is only death."

"You are barely fifty."

"How many specialists do you know who are as old as me?"

"Mack."

"He is younger."

"All right then, as an ancient specialist, tell me why there is no honor."

"Because all choices are evil, even the honorable ones. A truly honorable man knows this, and so I suppose you can say that Misha is honorable in this respect. But you ask the wrong man, Sergei. I am only an old specialist. Misha is the philosopher, especially since he won Alex; she is the true expert on deep things and has made him into a thinking man. I like good food, good wine, and beautiful, willing women. I cannot make love to an idea."

"And song," said Frank. "Don't forget song. Wine, women, and song."

Louis looked up from the rifle and grinned. He polished it absently with a chamois. "No. Charlie is the one for song. But I like a good joke. Philosophy is not funny. Tell me then, what is the most useless thing on a woman?"

"I don't know. What?"

"A babysitter."

"Very funny."

"I think so."

"If all choices are evil, Louis," said Sergei. "How does an honorable man determine his course?"

Louis considered this as he applied the oil. "I believe what Misha does.... You understand that I must speak of him as your hypothetical honorable man because I am not one. In my case, choices are always simple. I choose Lafitte over house wine, chateaubriand over hamburger, a pretty woman over an ugly one. I prefer to kill my enemy before he has the opportunity to kill me. I carefully collect any money anybody offers me to do what I would be doing anyway, which is killing my enemies. I am a simple man and cannot be used as a model in this discussion."

He pointed the cleaning rod upward, didactically, as though presenting an academic lecture. John fought to stay awake and listen. Frank snored.

"This is how Misha uses his honor," Louis instructed. "He determines his general position on any moral point before he is confronted with a specific case. He measures possibilities against a standard. Thus, he is at least consistent, if not always right. Only once was he overcome by emotion and it nearly killed us all. But in the end, he righted himself, and the problem was solved."

"After Ekaterina and Nadia were killed," said Sergei, "I determined never again to participate in the killing of innocents."

"Very noble." Louis reassembled the rifle and reached into the locker for another.

"Is it?"

"Yes. And you would see it as such if the woman you are trying to save were as blameless as little Nadia and if the man you are trying to save her from were not your excellent and lifelong friend. You are plagued by knowing everyone involved and nobody is fitting into your standards as they should. You can comfort yourself with the consolation of preventing death, which is always a good thing to do, but it is not quite true, is it? You have already killed two. Fortunately, you did not know them, so you are not haunted by the grief of their families."

They listened for a while to Frank's snores. Then Louis spoke more frankly. "There will be more deaths before we find the list, you know. If Mara is not one of those killed, what will be the acceptable toll to your honor? If she lives and Vladimir does not, how will honor help you? Be grateful to Misha for shortening your troubles, with whatever method he chooses."

"You are not helping me."

"I am your enemy Sergei Nickolaevich. I miss Vasily. I wish he were up on that other bunk, not this irritating doctor. I wish he were planning the charges that would get us safely into that warehouse. None of us can do it without blowing us all out of the solar system. Do not think I have any desire to help you."

"I can set the charges."

"What?" Louis stopped dismantling the new rifle and looked up at the bunk above him.

"I can set charges. Sobieski was my hero. I tried to copy everything he did, except killing. I had to be as much like him as I could to catch him."

Louis poked the barrel into the canvas over his head. "Shut up." He continued the job he was doing and made himself busy brushing the firing pin.

"A few years ago," Louis said finally, "Misha and I almost killed each other over Mara's mother, Alex. Details are not important, but Steve and Charlie kept us alive."

He looked up at John who peered down at him from the opposite high bunk, as unobtrusively as he could make himself.

"I will tell you Steve did not pull his punches with me as he does with you, Doctor."

He picked up the chamois and began polishing.

"Misha and I were babies together," he continued, "and there we were, fighting over a woman. After such a painful education, I learned, finally, that a wife is the completion of the self. It is possible to give up yourself for a friend, of course, but what true friend would require it? Misha forgave me. Alex learned to stay out of my way. If Volodya is a true friend, you will have no evil choice. If he is not, you have my permission, with glee, to shoot him."

Louis placed the reassembled rifles in the foot locker. He shoved the cleaning kit under his cot, where the bottle of oil tipped over and rolled around the room, leaking a drop at a time, adding to the odors.

John was hungry; he had not eaten since that long-ago breakfast. The scotch he'd sipped in Roger's room did not sit well on an empty stomach. Frank snored already. John stared at the ceiling, debating with himself the definitions of blameless and wife. The priest said, "Repeat after me," and John held up his gloved hands and said, "With these hands, I thee heal." Mara said something in Russian and John told himself he was dreaming.

TWENTY-ONE

It was a bad dream and waking was no better. John woke in the air on his way to the floor. Steve had him by the collar of Charlie's green polo shirt. John found his feet, stood, and prepared a reply—remarkably fast, he thought, through the grogginess. Why is the bastard smiling? And why doesn't he defend himself? These thoughts came swiftly, but John's fist would be faster. Another thought intruded. Something about Mack personally enforcing....

His fist never reached Steve's face, because he was spinning for some reason and then facing Mack, then hit with what was surely a battering ram. The familiar empty gasp for air resumed and he wondered if his spleen had ruptured. He flew down the aisle into Mara, who stepped aside at just the right time, and he fell at her feet. She helped him up, though he couldn't use the help, needed to breathe first, but somehow, he made it down the narrow aisle on his feet. He landed on his knees at the galley sink and fought the urge to hold his throbbing abdomen. He wished to God Mara was not watching.

"You're riding with me, Doc. Come on." Frank pulled the green shirt's collar further out of shape.

John stumbled to his feet to follow it, still not see-ing clearly. Vision and breathing did not clear until he sat in the passenger seat of the cab and Frank turned the key, then shifted into gear.

"You heard the brief, my beamish boy," said Frank. "Rule One. No alterc… no pugil… no fights. Mack will enforce it. You look a little ragged. Are you okay? You're okay. Mack knows how to break things and how not to. I don't think we're at breaking point just yet. It's coming though. You need to cool that temper of yours. Get that chip off your shoulder be-fore these guys knock your head off with it. Take it, it's good advice. Love, Frank." Frank made a smack-ing sound.

John carefully palpated his torso, looking for signs of rupture. Satisfied that everything was intact, he looked outside at the blackest night on the darkest road he'd ever seen.

"Where the hell are we?"

"We're on US 95 headed south to Las Vegas. We'll cross the Dam and pick up 93 to Phoenix, where we'll get on I-10 and stay there all the way to San Antonio. One thousand seven hundred miles of pure, bare-ass desert, except for the last few miles to San Antone. Thirty-two hours, not counting fuel stops, because we're extra heavy, which puts us at roughly six watches each before it's over, in which to get along with an increasingly wired team of killers in a small space, with a woman on board to add thrills and chills. God, I love it. Yes, indeedy speedy. There," he pointed to a black box on the console. "That's the GPS. Learn how to use it. I'm going to make you drive next, if Mack approves, to keep you out of trouble."

The box glowed green and amber. A series of numbers changed continually on a lighted display.

"What's a GPS?"

Frank whistled. "Global Positioning System. We use a satellite to tell our position. The numbers are latitude and longitude. As we head south, watch the lat numbers change, seconds and minutes. Jay gave us some primary and backup fuel stops roughly four hours apart. Punch this button," he pressed a switch on the left of the box, "for the next stop. The button on the right gives you a backup if that stop's not clear. Jay did his homework, the darling lad."

"Where is Jay?"

"He left us back on I-80, hoping to take her lady-ship, the lawyer esquirette, with him, but no luck. She and Roger are about a half mile behind us. I imagine we'll see Jay later, from time to time."

"You said fuel stops. What about food and a toi-let? That little marine toilet won't last more than a few more hours with all this coffee."

"Speaking of coffee," said Frank. "How about a cuppa?" He opened his bulgy eyes so that the whites glowed green in the dashboard lights.

Mack sat in a folding chair by the coffee pot, wearing the headset. John poured carefully, careful not to spill, careful not to get too close. The tape ma-chine started and stopped. Louis and Sergei played chess at the table. "Check," said Sergei. Louis glow-ered at him.

"About food," he reminded Frank when he hand-ed him the coffee.

"I don't know why you'd want any now," said Frank. "Don't think any of us will clean it up when you upchuck after getting hit in the gut. But if you insist, you can buy some during a fuel stop—if you get to go out on one. Otherwise, there are some high-energy bars in the coffee cabinet. Don't eat too many, though. The team will need them before they go out."

John wondered how to volunteer for a fuel stop. They would use the car for that, he knew. Maybe he could go with Mara. No. Wrong shift. "I don't have any money on me, Frank. How do I get paid for this?"

This. Now there was a whole host of questions. What, exactly, was this?

"Ah. Now there's a good question." Frank paused. "You see, my friend, money is always a good question, and this time partic... espe... certainly so. I have drawn the first half of the money offered for Pavlenko's hide to make it look good. But I am not a fool, no not me. I have the money sequestered and will return it when all this is over. Uncle Sam will forgive all manner of treason, but don't you even pretend to misappropriate a dime of his mullah or you will groom a golf course in some min-security federal hospitality cell for a very long time. I am not planning to retire that way. The team is funding this operation themselves. It costs plenty, but then, they have plenty, and evidently, they also have plenty of incentive this time. As for your salary, if Jay survives, and you survive, both ifs being questionable, maybe he can get the FBI to pay you. Maybe."

Great. John sipped his coffee.

"Another thing," resumed Frank. "If things do not go well, which is likely, but you have the misfortune to live, then when we are in court, please don't say you came along because you were chasing a pretty girl. It will not go over well. It will not go over at all. You say, my beamish, besotted boy, that you were threatened with death if you did not cooperate. It sounds good; it is the truth; and it will get you off."

"I haven't been threatened."

"Not aloud. It is assumed you can put two and two together. Always thought thinking was a requisite skill for medical school."

The coffee was good on a sore, empty stomach. The sky lightened a little on the left.

"What precisely, Frank," he said between sips, "am I cooperating in? I know about chasing girls, even though I've never been so damned unsuccessful before. When I get close, which is rare enough, I don't usually have the breath to speak to her. But the chase I understand. The rest, I don't."

Frank did not answer at first. He weighed his words, taking a long curve in the road with a leisurely swing of the wheel. Finally, he said, "Think of it in terms of what happens to Semianov's list. You know about the list, right?"

"A bunch of spies or something."

"Not just spies, my friend. Agents of influence. Deep cover illegals who influence different sectors of the country for purposes of disruption. Pavlenko says the list contains upwards of two hundred names. Of course, they are pernicious, but unlike your garden, home-grown variety of American critics, these have been cultivated, nurtured, and harvested by a foreign power, now defunct. Think about it. They will be highly placed, usually in government or communications, and a few in powerful industries. And none will resemble the so-called commies old Joe McCarthy tried to finger. I wouldn't be surprised if he was on that list.

Frank paused for an emotional gulp of his coffee. "Anyway, you have this list that everybody would like to see. I know I would. I know there are some in my chain, or I would not have been given the commission on Pavlenko. Twenty million is an enormous, desperate, number for one dead body."

He pointed down the road, as a visual aid to each point he wanted to make. "The options for this list, then, are these: it can fall into the hands of the listees. They will destroy it and carry on being disruptive. It can be captured by some wacky interest group and be published. God forbid."

"Why? Isn't that the best result?"

Frank sighed. "Look at all the factions in this country, Doc. Do you know anything about the right wing? No? Let me tell you it goes all the way around 'til it's back to being the left. On the way, you've got people convinced there's a worldwide conspiracy to occupy this country with Russkies and hippies. Won't they love the list?"

He warmed to his subject as his voice rose in pitch.

"Then there are the ones who think the white supremacists are the real people of God and to hell with the Jews. Then how about the black Muslim nationalists, eh? And all these people are armed. And so are the great big mass in the middle that doesn't know what the hell any of those isms are—except it's a plot against sacred capitalism—but knows damn well what a Russian spy is, by God." Frank struck the wheel with hand holding his cup and sloshed the last drops onto the dash.

"The cry will go up," he said with suitable drama. 'They're coming for our guns!' First anarchy, then tyranny, after lots and lots of blood. God help the group that isn't armed. It's called genocide. Let's not forget the larcenous and the criminals. The Skinheads, Crips, Bloods, and the various Mafias are all armed with more than handguns, my friend. Just think about the impact of a civil war on a country where the lottery is the only way a schmuck can get rich. Talk about a jackpot!"

"Who do you think will win in the end?"

"Hell, Doctor. I don't even know what side I'll be on, let alone what the end will be."

"So why are we trying to stop them from destroying the list? We should help them do it." John's cup was empty. He stared into the bottom of it, regretting its end.

Frank was patient. "If there is another copy, it can surface again. That's one danger. And the people we're talking about have already made a mess of one major power; they can repeat themselves here. That's the other danger. Jay has a better plan."

"Which is?"

"He will use the list to clean things up a bit. If another copy shows up, it will be old news. The country will yawn. Who cares? It's history. Last week is an ancient time in this country."

"How will Jay do that?"

"He'll Hoover it. Not the British version as in vacuum, but the American, as in J. Edgar. He'll arrange for some quiet resignations, a few retirements, maybe a career change or two, out of power, out of action, a few may go to jail. He thinks it will work."

"But you don't."

"If anybody can do it, Jay can. But I don't think anybody can do it. I think we'll be torn apart eventually. If Jay can save a few innocent lives in this case, I'll do what I can to help him. As for the guilty, I believe traitors should be shot. That's one of the things I don't like about Jay's plan, but then, he may have some plans along that line that I don't know about. Here's our stop."

John looked at the GPS. The numbers blinked at him. The sun was up now, already hot, in a flawless sky vaulted over brown rock-rubble hills. They pulled off the road at a public picnic table. There was shelter of a sort from a clump of mesquite and a trash can tilted on a stick, inviting use.

A hand reached through the black curtain and twisted John's shirt collar. A voice said, "*Kommen Sie.*" John obeyed without knowing the language, hating his shirt collar and its willingness to be used to order him about. Mack put a set of car keys in his hand as he pushed him out the door and back toward the green car.

"You drive."

TWENTY-TWO

"Turn left," said Mack.

John had signaled right. "Jay's map says to use the station on the right."

"They are going left."

"Who are going left?"

Mack pointed at a blue car ahead of them that John had not noticed, though he'd followed it up the exit ramp.

He shuddered at Mack's patience. The man's stillness did not reassure him. It was not kindly or understanding. Rather, it expressed without words how little John and his mistakes mattered. He thought about the big gun—called a sig-something wasn't it? —concealed under Mack's plaid flannel shirt. Who the hell cares what kind it is? The emergency room taught him that big guns make big holes in people. For the first time, he felt the menace. Until now, it was an intellectual curiosity, something that affected other people. Yes, he could die, but of course, he wouldn't. He was the hero of his own story; how could he die? Painfully. The ER had taught him that, too.

At the gas station, Mack worked the pump and kept watch in a complete circle, like a blue-eyed owl. Roger, the FBI man, poured gas into the blue Ford at the next pump. He fumbled, dropped the gas cap, and had to crawl under the car in his white shirt and maroon tie to retrieve it. He watched the blue-eyed man in the flannel shirt. He acknowledged John's friendly wave with a minimal nod but did not smile.

They were a happy party of four as they lined up to pay for the gas. John picked up a package of little donuts. Mack made him put it back.

"It will make you sick."

John tried to take a small bag of barbecue chips.

"It will make me sick," said Mack.

Judy made trouble, not in a conventional way, but simply by being her own loud, odious, and insensitive self. She stood behind Mack at the checkout, tugging at his sleeve while she smiled and insulted. She mentioned Mack's resemblance to Charlie and then talked about Mara. John heard the word 'bitch' all the way back at the door, where he and Roger watched each other and the cars.

"Get him the fuck outta here," said Roger through his teeth. He hardly moved his lips. The sound was lower than the last shelf of little donuts.

"What do I look like? Rambo?" John answered the same way.

"Aren't you a babysitter?"

"I'm a doctor. I don't even own a gun."

"No shit?"

Mack and Judy came toward them. Mack held her arm; she was strangely silent. He hit John in the chest with a fifty-dollar bill and said, "Pay this," then led the woman out the door and around a corner of the building.

Roger and John looked at each other and paid for their gas. John bought a package of little donuts. It made him sick almost immediately.

…

Louis wore the earphones and gave them a thumbs-up as they climbed into the RV. The tapes turned, top and bottom. Frank pointed John to the driver's seat. He was to drive—with Mack as his passenger.

The place swam in coffee, but he could not think about it. The little donuts played hockey in his stomach and John suppressed an urge to bring them up, though they were insisting. The drive was smooth and straight, from vanishing point to vanishing point, with occasional traffic ahead, a blue Ford following, rocks and scrubby bushes on either side. Mack watched his face.

"Frank," said Mack, "bring the doctor some coffee."

Frank's hairy arm pushed through the curtain with a Styrofoam cup at the end of it. John forced some down and to his surprise, the donuts were tamed.

"I like this desert," said Mack. "I can see a long way."

John searched for conversational topics. He rejected golf, sailing, investments, girls, parties, colleges. Any discussion of the weather would be over in one word, hot. Politics and religion—*dear God, big guns make big holes in people.*

"When do you think we'll be finished?" he said. It was the best he could do.

"Why?"

Because I need to stay awake and conversation is a means to that end and maybe after you have that list, I can get close enough to ask her for a phone number.

"I have a meeting tomorrow," is what he said aloud.

"You will not be there. What meeting?" In his way, Mack was making conversation.

"The Medical Ethics Committee."

"And what are medical ethics? What large questions do you discuss in this meeting?"

John shrugged. "The usual. Things like a doctor's responsibilities to the patient and his family? That sort of thing."

"And what are your responsibilities?"

John glanced at Mack as he scanned the horizon. There were lines at the sides of his eyes, deep circles underneath. His day-old beard formed a shadow over his cheeks and chin. Everybody had this shadow. No one had shaved. Mack's beard was blond and thick, like his hair, with scattered strands of gray that disappeared in some lights. He raised an eyebrow, waiting for an answer.

"I follow the Hippocratic oath," said John. "Above all, I must do no harm. I don't have a problem with the obvious cases."

"Do no harm? What were you planning to do with your fist this morning?"

John resisted an urge to whine about Steve's wake-up methods. He said nothing.

"And what about cases that are not obvious?" said Mack. "Tell me what is not obvious."

"Cases," John began slowly, "like a bypass on a bedridden eighty-six-year old because the hospital needs to boost profits or scraping a fungus infection from the sinuses of a terminal three-year-old cancer patient. The question is, how much abuse should you inflict on a body in an effort to save it?"

Mack did not speak for five minutes, at least. John gave up on the conversation and kept himself awake with what remained of his coffee. He suppressed the growing need to relieve himself and looked at the numbers as they danced incomprehensibly on the GPS. When he glanced up, he noticed Mack watching him.

John was surprised when Mack spoke again.

"No files, Frank."

A voice came from behind the curtain. "I know, Mack. I know."

"The only way to stop Frank from listening is to kill him. It is too late for that now. I should have shot him years ago. I will tell you a story. No files, Frank."

"Yes, sir. No files."

John waited.

"It vass," Mack stretched as he began, so that his accent became heavier than usual, and the words hissed. He yawned. "It was more than twenty years ago, I think, that Frank asked us to stop a terrorist team in Chicago. They planned to blow up a large building, killing hundreds, perhaps thousands. They met an obstacle, which delayed them and delayed us in killing them. We found a girl who could clear their obstacle, and so help us to kill them, and I decided to use her. She would die, of course, but the alternative was hundreds dead and a very loud explosion."

He scanned the horizon continuously. "Coffee, Frank, though I am soaked in it. And for the doctor."

John did not know where he would put it, but coffee had become a primary joy in his life, and he accepted it.

"Did you use the girl?" he asked when he heard Frank settle on the folding chair behind the curtain.

"Yes, of course." Mack sipped his coffee. "The girl was younger than Mara is now, about twenty years. She was unremarkable, typical, and ordinary American bourgeois, not as beautiful as Mara, but pretty enough, I suppose. She had too much brown hair that would not stay put, and she was small, insignificant.

We hated each other from the first moment. She thought she knew all about good and evil and I was the next thing to Lucifer. She agreed to help us without understanding what that meant. Her goodness grated on me, or else I would not have thought more than a moment about killing her to save so many, but I knew that my dislike could affect my judgment. So I thought about it."

Mack paused long enough for John to contemplate prompting him with word *and?* He restrained himself.

"It was the right thing to do," Mack said finally.

Did the words suffer from too much emphasis? Like he needed to convince himself?

"Vasily's judgment also was affected by this girl," he continued. "He loved bourgeois American girls and this one smiled at him, giggled at his jokes, ran to him in her troubles. It was disgusting. He pleaded with me for her to have a chance, any chance. I pointed out that to give her a chance would probably result in her torture, and after all, a chance is only a chance.

"'No matter,' said Vasily. 'A chance is still a chance, and torture does not matter.'"

Mack's voice softened in both tone and volume. John glanced at him as he stared down their endless road into his past—into his friend's past.

"Now understand, Doctor," he said, "Vasily was an expert on torture. He blew up communist party meetings with his uncles in Poland when he was fifteen and had been interrogated already when Louis and I took him from a prison in Gdansk at eighteen. After that, there were many more times. Even his mother died under interrogation.

"Vasily was an expert; he wanted the girl, and he was my friend. I could not refuse him."

Breathless and appalled, John had to ask, "What happened?"

"I devised a plan that required her to give the terrorists only part of what they needed. They would ask her for the rest. We dressed her as a harlot, to give her a legend and to ease the interrogation. If they were busy and unimpressed by her, we thought, they might not hurt her sexually. But…"

What must have been a painful memory made the man wince. John dared not insist he spit it out. Instead, he kept his eyes on the road and sipped his cooling coffee until Mack continued.

"She was a virgin and I do not know anyone who does not check these things, even inadvertently when looking for weapons. She was also completely naive. She cried whenever I came near her. We could not send her to interrogation that way, so Louis suggested she should not be a virgin. I agreed, but Vasily would not take the responsibility. He could not hurt her, he said."

Mack sighed. "So, I told her to choose one of us. We knew she preferred Vasily, but she would not choose. She would not participate in any way in such an evil as sex. Imagine it. I am surrounded by so much goodness and nobility, that it falls to me to essentially rape the girl. It was all very civilized. The girl survived. Both me and the interrogation."

"So you are saying we should do whatever is medically necessary?" John said after another long pause.

Mack drained his cup, crushed it, and threw it through the black curtain. "I am saying nothing. I am a killer, not a healer. I do not know what is 'medically necessary.' Also, I have not finished the story. Louis! Frank is not taking notes?"

"No notes. I will shoot him if I see paper."

"*Vielen Dank!*"

John forced the last drop of his coffee down his throat. He threw the cup behind him without crushing it, and really, really needed to pee.

"You do not know what it is like during an operation, Doctor, during my kind of operation. There is a great calm. Even the weapons you fire make their noise as if they are a long way off. Time becomes very slow, because in the next moment, for you anyway, time may end, and it is certainly ending for those around you, those you are shooting, those shooting next to you. It is no different with a knife, or with killing by hand. All your senses are concentrated on killing before you are killed. During the operation in Chicago, one of the tangos..."

"Tangos?"

"Terrorists. One of them took this girl and like the coward he was, used her to shield himself from me. I kicked her out of the way, breaking her ribs. Do you follow this? She has been raped, tortured, and now beaten, but she is alive because Vasily wants her. He has pleaded for her."

It was an emotional narrative, spoken without drama, a post-operative report without reference to the soul within the sutured body. In the next breath, it became even more matter-of-fact.

"The enemy disarmed me. He was a good fighter. We fought with knives, toe to toe, rolling on the floor. He was much bigger than me, at least a hundred twenty kilos. In a fight like that, skill does not matter. Strength always wins. Using all my strength, I could not keep his knife from my throat. I held his wrist, with the point only a centimeter from my carotid. I had my knife in the other hand, but there was no room to maneuver; he was on top of me."

Again, his voice dropped.

"Then this insignificant, silly, bourgeois American girl found my gun on the floor, picked it up by the barrel, and hit a one hundred twenty kilo killer on the head with it. Tap. Like this." He tapped the dashboard in front of him. "Nothing. Less than useless. Except that for a fraction of time, and in slowed time that is a very long time you understand, he loosened his grip on my other hand. I was able to turn my knife and pull, disemboweling him.

"Louis and Vasily had not been completely successful, and I was needed to catch another man who had the means to destroy the building. I caught him."

John waited.

"I thought I would save hundreds by letting one die," said Mack, "when that one saved me, and by doing so, also those hundreds. And only because Vasily pleaded for her."

"So you would never again make a decision like that, to sacrifice one for many?"

"What? Don't be stupid. Of course, I would. It was the right decision. First comes the objective and the life of my team. Everything else is insignificant. Always."

John's exasperation came through in his voice. "Then what is your point?"

"Typical American. You must have everything spelled out for you. The point is that no agonized decision will do away with pain and death. These are inevitable. The question is, is there someone who will plead for you?"

Was Mack asking him? John stared back at him until the RV began to drift.

"The girl who saved your life," John said, "you said she hated you."

"Yes. She did. Almost to the day she agreed to marry me."

TWENTY-THREE

Seal thought the damn rules could be lifted just this once. He thought it while he watched the other shift raid the fridge and grab themselves each a cold one. He licked his lips. Mara handed him a cup of coffee. He glared at Charlie when he burned the roof of his mouth, glared until Charlie turned around, that is, being smart enough to douse the challenge before Charlie saw it.

There would be entertainment this shift change, Louis's treat, an audio performance featuring Roger and Judy in star roles as themselves. Louis changed the reels, gave Seal the headphones to monitor current taping, and cued up the old tape for playback. People scrambled for seats.

The doctor missed his chance because he was too busy complaining. He started on the smell, then some nonsense about hygiene, and finally the heat, and what about...? Steve popped Louis's beer open under the doctor's nose. The doc shook his beer and spewed it over Steve. Mack was at his elbow, so Steve did not liquefy the good doc but settled for flipping him the bird. Busy with their private feud, they were both late when Mara came in and sat in the booth seat with her back to the sink. Pavlenko scooted in next to her. The doctor was quick enough to sit across the table, and Steve sat next to him, across from Pavlenko.

Charlie opened a folding chair and sat next to Steve. Mack shoved Frank out of another chair and set it up near the door so he could watch the sensor screens. All outside sensors were on, both camera and infrared. The Frenchman watched, too, from a standing position near the comm bank. Frank huddled on the locker in the back corner. He may be huddled, thought Seal, but he sure is happy. Frank had a big shit-eating grin on his face. *He has scored some major intel.*

Seal stood behind the sink, where he had a great view of everybody, including Sergei Pavlenko's hand as it reached for Mara's. She pulled hers away. He reached again and she let him hold on. The two testosterone-enriched competitors across from them could not see through the table, but Seal noticed that Mack was in direct line of sight on Pavlenko's right. Pavlenko was a brave man.

The Frenchman gave the signal, Seal pressed the button, and the show began.

"This is what we heard after you met Roger and his lawyer at the fuel stop," Louis told Mack.

The first voice was Roger's. "Jeez Louise, Judy, you gotta stop."

"That man is dangerous, Roger. You should arrest him. Quick, before they get away."

"They aren't getting away. They are none of our business. The office said that since Frank Cardova is with them, we're out of it. We're supposed to follow Turner."

"You follow my orders."

"Jeez Louise."

"These men are up to something."

"Whatever they're up to, we don't want to know about it, Judy. Listen. This stuff is called WEDGE, okay? It's a compartmentalized caveat. I saw it on the boss's desk. It's got stripes and bars and whistles all over the folder. We're not cleared for it. It's classified beyond Mars, and we got no rockets."

"Then how do you know this is WEDGE? What does WEDGE stand for, anyway?"

"I've heard rumors, bar talk. Shit. I've got a wife and three kids and another one due in December and I want to go back to bank robbery. It's safer. I don't know why I moved to counter-terror. I wanted a smart boss for a change, I guess, and Turner's the smartest there is, but he winds up under investigation himself, and now I have to drive us to San Antonio, while you do your best to get us killed. Killed, Judy. Dead, as in doornail, ding-dong dead.

"We're supposed to follow Turner, a nice easy assignment. He practically invites us to ride with him, but no, you get yourself pu... no that doesn't work... dick whipped by Steve what's-his-name, and I know in my bones he is a killer. He's got the eye, the bearing, and I've heard some rumors, like I said. So we follow him and come up on another character I think I've heard about, and you go and make a scene with him."

"I resent this, Roger. That man took me behind the station and threatened me with a knife. I could have been killed, or worse. It's a good thing I'm wearing a gun."

The RV erupted in laughter.

In the background, Roger's voice on the tape came through, "Jeez Louise. Jeez Louise. A knife. Jeez Louise, it is the one. Judy, that one will cut your throat before you get your hand to your holster. He can cross a twenty-foot space and kill with a knife before most people—even the best—can draw their guns. Let's go back and see if we can pick up Turner's trail."

"No way. These guys are up to something, and I want to know what it is. Something is going on in San Antonio, and we have a sworn duty to uphold the law. Besides, Steve could never kill anybody. He's so gentle and sweet."

The Frenchman doubled over in laughter.

"You've seen a lot more of him than I have, Jude, that's for sure," said Roger. "How many scars does he have? What gun does he carry?"

"Hmm?" She paused. "Oh, it's nice and big."

Seal had never laughed so hard. Mack laughed, a very rare sight. Frank fell off the locker. Charlie punched Steve in the arm. Steve's face turned a deep magenta. Mara covered her face with both hands as she laughed. Steve snuck in a punch to Doc's ribs during the ruckus. The doctor laughed anyway.

The Frenchman and Frank had just picked themselves up off the floor when Judy said, "Roger, you don't think they know we're following them?"

Behind the laughing din, the tape player squawked, "Jeez Louise."

In a high, squeaky voice, Steve said, "Help me, help me. I'm stupid and I can't get up."

Frank fell off the locker again, crawled to the refrigerator, and sat with his back to the side of it while he opened another beer.

At Louis's signal, Seal stopped the machine. Frank was told to break out another round for his watch. He was handing them over pretty freely and Seal almost succeeded in taking one until he felt Charlie's eyes on him, like fucking laser beams burning right through from front to back, the son of a bitch, and he put his hand up to his head and smoothed back his hair over the top, pretending it was what he had his arm out for all along. Charlie didn't let go his surveillance on Seal until Frank threw the can at the doctor. Steve caught it, shook it, and sprayed it over the doc.

As usual, the doctor was losing when Louis called for quiet. "Fun is over," he said. "We return to the game." He nodded at Seal.

The tape turned again, and Roger and Judy talked about Jane.

"Funny," said Judy, "she's just like Charlie. They're made for each other. Anybody warm-blooded would lose skin if they touched them. Like licking an icicle in zero degrees. Isn't it strange how she's so beautiful and Jay Turner's so ugly, yet they're both black?"

"What the hell's strange about that?" said Roger. "It's only strange if you don't see them as people."

"I've won some important affirmative action cases. Of course, I see African-Americans as people."

Roger did not answer.

Seal squashed an urge to say 'Jeez Louise' aloud.

"She's going to San Antonio, you know," said Judy. "She told me she's driving out in a van. I saw her back at the exit off I-80."

"You didn't tell me that."

"I waved, but she ignored me. I figured it was because she wasn't with Charlie. Then I forgot about it."

"What was she driving?"

"It was a green van, but the guy she was with was the one driving."

"What kind of van? What guy?"

"I don't know! A big van. I never saw the guy before. White guy. Long hair, kind of dirty blond. He had a mustache and one of those all the way across eyebrows. Who do you think he was?"

Seal stopped the tape, and Louis brought out a manila file folder with an eight-by-ten glossy taped inside. He opened it and displayed a picture of a man with sand-colored hair, a mustache, and prominent eyebrows.

"We want to watch for a large, green van," he said. "We have all seen Jane Jared. This is Vladimir Dimitrovich Maximovich, her babysitter."

"If you see them," Mack said to Charlie and Steve, "do not hesitate. Take them out."

Charlie nodded and studied the coffee in his Styrofoam cup. Pavlenko drained his beer.

TWENTY-FOUR

The party broke up. Seal adjusted his headphones. Louis dragged out a footlocker full of rifles, submachine guns, and gun cleaning supplies. Charlie told Steve to drive and Mara to ride in the cab as passenger. You could read the disappointment on the doctor's face, but before he could escape to a bunk, Charlie said, "Sit down, John. Then, "Get some sleep, Louis. The doctor volunteers to stay up this shift. I'll clean the weapons."

Louis reached for the ceiling and steadied himself as the RV accelerated onto the highway. He looked at Charlie, who was already laying a cleaning kit out on the table. "Hesitation kills," he told him.

"I know," said Charlie. "I will not hesitate. Get some sleep."

It was just the three of them, Seal on the machine, Charlie cleaning guns, and the doctor trying to figure out what to do with himself. They could hear Steve and Mara talking quietly in the cab.

The doctor poured himself a cup of coffee. "What are they saying?" He mumbled the question to Seal, throwing his head over his shoulder in the direction of the cab.

Seal shrugged. "No Deutsch here, Doc. I did French and Spanish."

The doctor sat back down at the table, across from Charlie, who rammed a cleaning rod through a barrel. John picked up a full magazine, studied it, and put it down. He looked at one of the submachine guns in front of him and reached a hand toward it.

"Don't touch it," said Charlie, without looking up.

John put both hands under the table. He cleared his throat. "What sort of a gun is this one?" He pointed with his chin.

Seal marveled at how stupid a smart man could be. Of course, the man was tired, but somebody should tell him about starting conversations with working specialists during an op. Working specialists with loaded weapons. Every magazine on the table was full; most of the guns held full magazines. The one next to Charlie had a round chambered. Seal saw him chamber it. He should tell the doctor to shut up. He should, but he wasn't about to.

To Seal's surprise, Charlie answered John's question. "That is an H&K MP5 SD3 submachine gun." His voice was almost conversational. Almost.

"Oh." The doctor nodded as if that meant something to him. "What kind of bullets does it use?"

"Nine-millimeter."

"Oh. How big is that?"

Charlie stared at him. He couldn't believe it, either. He put the cleaning rod and barrel down, picked up a stray magazine, and took out a round. He handed it to the doctor. "That big," he said.

"The front is empty."

"We use hollow point."

John turned it over in his hand. "I've heard that word in the ER. It makes big holes in people. How many of these can that gun shoot in a minute?"

"Why do you want to know?"

John shrugged. Charlie reassembled the now clean weapon.

"What about that big one in front of you?" The doc was at it again. He pointed at a beautiful sniper rifle stretched across the table in front of Charlie. Seal shook his head.

Charlie stopped again and stared at the doc. "It's mine."

"What kind is it?"

"It was custom-made for me. In Ferlach."

"Is that a scope on top? Can it shoot pretty far?"

"Yes. It's a stainless steel, thirty-two power, all-weather scope. The range is adequate."

Master of understatement.

"How far does it shoot?"

"Why do you want to know?"

"Why are you so secretive?"

There was a long pause. Seal pinched himself to stop a loud guffaw.

"How long have you worked for the FBI, John?" asked Charlie. He reloaded the now clean MP5.

"I don't work for them. I'm on a retainer. For emergencies."

"How many other emergencies have you been called to?"

"None."

"How much training did they give you before they put you on standby?"

"Training? I'm a board-certified surgeon."

"How much intelligence training?"

"Oh. That. I've seen all the James Bond movies." John grinned.

In Seal's experience so far, Charlie had no appreciable sense of humor. Like his father, he was more stable than the wild and woolly Frenchman or Steve Donovan, but he was also less likely to smile at anything.

Charlie casually put down the MP5, muzzle pointed at John. "I saw three of those movies," he said.

"Do you notice that all of the women are beautiful, cooperative, and benign, all at the same time? If you find one of those here, tell me. Also, Bond's bruises, if he gets any, heal right away. Did you know your eye is the color of French mustard?"

Unspoken, but unmistakable: Do you want the other eye to match it? No? Then shut up.

Maybe it was because he was on Charlie's watch, so he saw a lot of the man, but Seal had become increasingly careful around him, more so than with any of the others, even Mack. Charlie was more than just a chip off the old block. The father observed people. Charlie measured them. Mack threatened; Charlie targeted. The older man was in the game; the son was in the business, and his business was no fuss, no muss, killing. The amazing thing was that the Jared woman had managed to move this one. After her, he was not likely to be moved again.

Immunized forever against intruders, thought Seal.

"Seal," said Charlie.

Seal jumped.

"There are packages of new rope under the body armor in the shower, and there's a box of hooks in the corner on the right. Get those. Bring them here."

Seal noticed it was becoming easier to squeeze between the refrigerator and the sink. The thought made him hungry.

"Do you know how to tie knots?" Charlie asked the doctor, waylaying him in front of the toilet before he could go to the back and lie down.

John nodded.

"I want knots like this." Charlie took a rope end, looped and knotted it through the eye of a hook, and handed it to him. "Untie it and let me see you do it again. Good. Do sixteen of those. Then run every rope through your fingers, the entire length, and look for flaws or frays."

"They're brand new."

"It doesn't matter. Look at every inch. Disasters start with stupid things, like weak ropes."

"What do you use all this rope for?"

"Getting from high places to low places quickly and vice versa."

"Are you going to do that in San Antonio?"

"Maybe. We may have to go in through the roof."

"But you don't know?"

Charlie studied him. "Pavlenko has not yet told us everything."

"Why not?"

"He wants to stay alive a little longer."

John turned the hook over in his hand, scowling. "Is this some kind of plastic?" he asked.

"It's titanium. Now shut up and work on top of the table, where I can see your hands."

The doctor worked quietly, almost as if he understood the threat.

Roger and Judy said little in Seal's ear, only an occasional "Jeez Louise" that made the tape roll. It was like any other mind-numbing stake-out except for the discomfort of Charlie's presence. These were fast shifts, only four hours instead of twelve or sixteen, and this one was nearly half over. Seal thought Steve was pulling over for the midway fuel stop.

But then Steve called out through the black curtain. "I see a green van."

TWENTY-FIVE

I was at the top of my class, of all my classes, John thought as he ran the rope between his fingers. That was not somebody else; I was the one who graduated summa cum laude. These are thugs, killers, spooks, experts in pain and mayhem. They are no better than a street gang. They are frightening only because they are a little smarter—in their field. A lot smarter. They are summa cum laude killers.

The summa cum laude killers were looking at the computer on the refrigerator. They punched in their position from the GPS, and the screen gave them a three-dimensional topographical map of the area. Arizona? Did it say Arizona? When did they pass Las

Vegas? Hoover Dam? What did you see on your drive across the country, John? *Guns, fists, rope, and coffee.*

The map showed another side road on the left, about a quarter of a mile down the highway, parallel to the road where Steve saw the green van. How far down was the van? Charlie wanted to know. Half a kilometer, Steve told him. Mara drove. John touched the rope as he pulled it through his hands. He had good fingers; he felt every irregularity. He was a surgeon.

It did not occur to him that the green van meant anything more than a confused account of a beautiful woman he had met briefly and some Russian guy he had never met and did not particularly want to meet.

On the side road, Mara turned the RV around so that it faced back toward the highway and then cut the engine. She turned on all the infrared sensors and cameras. The screens over John's head lit up. He sat with the rope still in his hand.

Steve came out of the back room with a black nylon bag. It was full of new packages of camouflaged clothing, boots, pants, shirts, and T-shirts, in khaki, tan, and sage green, in muted, blended shades, like the desert outside. Charlie brought body armor out of the shower.

"Shit, not the full armor, Charlie," said Steve. "It's fucking a hundred and twenty out there."

It was approaching the same inside.

"Okay. Soft body armor and no t-shirts. Hurry."

John sat with his mouth open, rope in his hand, as the two men stripped to their underwear.

"John, get off your ass and help Mara," said Steve.

John dropped the rope and stood next to Mara. She climbed onto a folding chair and pulled wires and gadgets from behind the radios above the cab. She handed them down as she found them. When John had a handful, she got down from the chair and took them away from him, one by one. She put an earpiece in Steve's left ear as he buttoned a pair of camouflaged trousers. A small, stiff wire with a thickened end extended over his chin. She bent it so that it rested under his lower lip, ran the wire leading from there down and over the Velcro shoulder of his body armor, and attached it to a small oblong box. This she clipped to a web belt he had just buckled around his waist. She took another wire and box from John and did the same for Charlie.

Mara gave Seal a wire and box, equipped herself with one, and finally set another up for John while he watched, dumbfounded, as Charlie and Steve completed their outfits with long-sleeved desert-cammie shirts and carryall vests made of sage green mesh. Into pockets and loops in the mesh went binoculars, knives, and an assortment of full magazines from the table and from their shoulder holsters, now discarded. Their handguns went into holsters on the web belts. They put on camouflaged hats with soft brims and covered their faces, ears, necks, and hands with tubes of black, brown, and green face paint. Steve picked up an MP5, checked the magazine, and chambered a round. Charlie picked up another MP5 and the long rifle with the scope. He handed the MP5 to Mara.

"Shoot him if he moves wrong," he told her. Still pointing to John, he said, "You can help her watch the screens." To Seal, "Don't wake anybody until I tell you."

Seal nodded. Everybody turned on their gadgets. Mara turned John's on for him, all the while keeping the muzzle of the submachine gun pointed at him.

John watched the screen as the two men moved up a slope and onto the top of a ridge. They stopped about a thousand feet away and blended in, disappearing when they didn't move.

"What are they doing?" John asked Mara.

She put a finger to her lips.

"But what's going on?"

"Shut the fuck up, John." It was Steve's voice coming straight into his left ear.

"We have a rendezvous, here," came Charlie's voice. "Green van, white van. There's Maximovich. There's Jared. There are one, two, three…I make it seven others. They're transferring equipment. Looks like….Shit… since when do Russians spring for MP5's? John, go get Pavlenko. Don't wake my father."

The words were flattened by the radio. John did not realize his name had been spoken until Mara nudged him.

When Pavlenko was properly wired, Charlie briefed him on the view. "What the hell kind of team is this, Sergei?"

"Describe them."

"Two about Steve's height, dark hair. Tattoos. Three are taller. One is huge. The seventh appears to be the driver."

"The huge one, is he heavily tattooed?"

"Yes."

"Sounds like Drakhiz. I thought he was released from service two years ago. Who is he working for?"

"What the hell kind of team is this?" Charlie insisted.

Sergei hesitated. He looked at Mara and swallowed hard. "It is an extraction team."

There was a pause. "Seal, wake the others."

"They're already here," said Seal.

TWENTY-SIX

Mara stood in her underwear, donned soft body armor and shifted it upward while Seal adjusted the Velcro at the shoulder.

Misha and Louis were only slightly ahead of her. They wore camouflaged trousers. Frank frantically tried to untangle a pair of wires.

Sergei untied a knot in the wires, then sat at the table with his forehead in his hand. John sat across from him, his mouth open, trying to watch Mara without looking at her. Her jog-bra and panties covered more than any bikini she might wear to a swimming pool, and he was a doctor for heaven's sake.

She did not have time to think any more about it.

They created a plan while Misha and Louis dressed and conducted the conversation over the radio speaker wedged above the cab.

Misha said, "It is your call."

"I want to hit them now." Michael's voice held some urgency.

"There is a risk. Odds are four to nine."

There was a pause. Then Michael: "*Numquam periclum sine periclo vincitur.* I want to use Mara. That makes it four and a half to nine."

Hah!

Misha looked at her and pointed to the bag of desert clothing. Start changing. It took him a little longer to say "Yes," out loud.

Mara dropped her indignation at her brother's jibe along with her jeans and rummaged through the bag for a shirt and pants. Seal brought her soft body armor from the shower.

There was one more message from Michael.

"We will use Wounded Wing. Mara will be *Vögelein*.

Louis was dressed and ready. He dug a Škorpion machine pistol out of the weapons locker.

Mara reviewed Wounded Wing procedures. She reviewed the sequence, the hand signals, and the movements. It would be on a downward slope, on the other side of the ridge. She ran her memory back to the basement under Vasily's Carpet and went over once again the instructions that echoed in the work-out room during all those cold mornings.

After her father's death, Mara had trained in earnest, never missing a session until she went to college. At first, they were reluctant to teach her all of it, but the little she knew had already saved her life, twice. They reasoned that it could not hurt her to know the weapons and techniques. Steve brought her to black belt. Michael sharpened her shooting. Misha taught her to think, Louis, to react. She was present when they developed and practiced new tactics. She knew the hand language, the radio codes, the operational disciplines.

Louis chambered a round in the Škorpion, folded back the stock, and put it on the table in front of her.

Seal hooked the radio onto the web belt around her waist. Mara stuffed another twenty-round magazine for the Škorpion into a pouch in the belt.

She reviewed signals again, unconsciously moving her fingers and hands. Misha caught her eye.

Stop. Not in front of the babysitters. It was a private language.

John began to babble something. He was protesting, by the whiny sound of it, and it threatened to break her concentration, but it didn't succeed. She thought, briefly, that Misha was pushing him back into the booth by the table to make him quiet, but that wasn't it. John's hand had come too near the Škorpion. Misha was being careful.

Louis untied her hair and piled it on top of her head under a soft-brimmed hat. Lose the hat on the way down. She nodded.

They tied Pavlenko to the sink before they left.

Seal gave her what he called positive encouragement. "Don't fuck up," he said.

...

The discussions were over. The endless philosophical debates ended under a desert sun on a blazing afternoon somewhere in Arizona. Mara moved up the ridge with Misha and Louis on either side of her.

When is it proper to kill? Under what circumstances? What is the morality of defending oneself? When does defense end and become aggression?

Was there a debating point about hitting a team of six killer kidnappers before they could hit you? The only discussable question was, How? By offering a target they would be tempted to take rather than kill outright. That could be only Mara. Misha had said yes. His lifetime of regrets and reservations had no place on an operation. There were no more philosophical questions. How do we hit them quickly, within range, and without getting hit ourselves? How do we avoid leaving a secondary target behind us?

At the top of the ridge, Michael moved Misha to the far right, then Louis next to him. Mara was to take the center, with Steve to her left and Michael on the far left. Michael pointed out their positions behind boulders on the other side of the ridge, and they moved into them silently.

Mara waited at the top with Michael. He had pointed his rifle at a spot two hundred meters down the slope. Here was where he expected the enemy to set up their covering fire. Maximovich and his team were still transferring equipment from the green van to the white one. There was a driver in the white van. In the passenger window of the green van, Mara saw a slender arm, Jane's arm.

When the others were in place, Michael pointed to the spot where he wanted her to land. He gave her the signal, Go.

Mara crept over the top of the ridge and down the other side. She used brush and rocks for cover until she was about fifteen meters from her desired position. She saw Steve crouching behind a boulder on her left, Louis was farther to the right. She was too far left, but there was no way to correct it, and anyhow, she was ready. Now.

Her foot dislodged a medium-sized rock and sent it rolling down the hill, a shower of pebbles and wannabe boulders following like groupies in its wake. She left the MP5 in the rubble and slid down with the stones, left leg straight, taking the abrasions on the right hip and shoulder, but keeping the Škorpion tucked up in the small of her back with her right hand. The hat was harder. It wanted to stay with her. She tossed her head and scraped the hat off on a dead piece of twisted brush as she passed it. Her blonde hair flew around her head.

She stopped sliding less than a meter to the left of where Michael had pointed. Not bad. She rubbed her left ankle, looked worriedly at the vans, and then scanned up over her shoulder to the top of the ridge. As she swept her eyes back around to the road below, she gave a desperate, despairing look to the MP5 lying out of reach above her.

I should get an Oscar.

She could see Steve out of the corner of her eye and sensed Louis and Misha on her right. She watched the extraction team put their hasty plan into action. They leapfrogged up the slope, four and two, covering as they ran, crouching, careful not to hit her. She gazed up at the ridge as if looking for help from there.

Michael fired an MP5 from the top, first from the right, then from the left, acting like four people everywhere at once, giving the impression that her defenders were pinned down. When the enemy fighters came within effective range of the top, two of them blasted the ridge, while the other four crawled toward Mara.

Michael was right. The fighters providing cover had crouched behind boulders two hundred meters down. Only their eyes and muzzles showed over the tops. Not much, but enough for Michael.

She waited. The four coming up the hill did not fire. They moved quickly on all fours. A big man with tattoos looked up at her and grinned.

"*Sofort*," said Michael's voice in her ear.

She rolled off the Škorpion, brought it up, and pulled. The big man reeled with the impact on his body armor and began to teeter backward. She adjusted for height, and he toppled as his head jerked back from the impact. She felt a shower of something wet. Blood, but not from the one she killed. It came from one closer whose head disintegrated under Steve's fire. There was noise all around her: the silenced MP5s, loud enough at ten meters despite the earplugs she wore and the crack-boom of Michael's rifle, the impacts and the death rattles and inert masses sliding through loose gravel. First one, then the other covering sniper fell silent. Another of Michael's precise rounds traveled at almost a thousand meters per second into the gas tank of the white van, exploding it on impact. The green van's armored tank did not explode, though Michael hit it repeatedly even when it was more than a thousand meters away on its way out.

"*Zurück*!" said Michael, and they turned and ran up the ridge and over the top.

They covered their backs one at a time while Michael spoke to the RV.

"John, start the truck. Frank, status."

"Normal." Frank's voice was calm.

"I want to see John climb into the cab, Frank. Move him."

Louis and Misha checked the blind side, then piled in through the door behind Michael, Steve, and Mara.

The engine was running, but John stood at the curtain to see her come in.

"Go, damn it! Frank, move him!"

Frank turned the doctor around roughly and shoved him back into the driver's seat.

Steve pulled a bottle of water from the refrigerator. The sleeves of his shirt were soaked to the hems and the wetness hugged his biceps. The soaking on his left hand ran pink with mingled blood and sweat. He drank most of the bottle and poured the rest over his face.

Misha cut the ropes that bound Sergei and, with Louis, carried him to the table where they laid his torso backward across it lengthwise, legs stretched toward the door, feet scrabbling among crushed coffee cups. This was the true panic, the lost look, that exceeded even his first sight of Steve and Charlie in the motel room. Mara turned away and saw Michael come out of the back room with a long, black device with a switch, a dial, and two metal ends.

She turned to the coffee pot, found her hair pins and rubber band, and busied herself with these, hands shaking because, oh God, she did not want to watch.

TWENTY-SEVEN

The knot in John's stomach was more than a hunger pain; it was a visceral twisting of his universe. The smell came in ahead of the team.

"What's that smell?" John asked.

"Cordite." Frank said it quietly, almost in his ear.

The team was not quiet. For the past fifteen minutes they had been eerily silent up there on that ridge, but now they were all noise, all movement, loud, violent, invading. Mara, too. And there was blood on her arm. John looked carefully but saw no source. It was not her blood. Steve was spattered with it and again, no source.

He had no time to observe more. He could feel Charlie's eyes on him and Charlie's impatience and Charlie's authority, even before Charlie said a word. Frank did not have to push so hard; he was already on his way back to the cab.

John drove toward the highway, then took the on-ramp and headed for Phoenix. The glaring sun hurt his eyes, made them water and squint and he did not see any green van, ahead or behind or to the side, or in the air, for that matter. Frank rode as his passenger and could look for it himself if it was so damned important.

"What language is that?" asked John. He was trying to concentrate on the sounds behind them.

"Russian."

"Do you understand it? What are they saying?"

"Steve is telling Pavlenko that Drakhiz is no more. They got all six of the extraction team and the driver."

"Got?"

Frank nodded, held up his hand, and listened. He spoke again. "Jared and her babysitter got away. Steve's Russian has improved since he worked for me."

"He worked for you?"

"He was a babysitter. Once."

Seal came through the curtain. His smell announced him. Where was he getting the food to spill on that shirt?

"You don't fit here," said Frank.

Seal made himself fit, between the seats and the GPS console. He laid the curtain over his back, bulging the shape, but keeping it closed. He steadied himself by pushing up the ceiling.

"I gotta be here, Frank. I can't be there. They got an iron, Frank. I can't watch. The girl took my earphones for me. Bless her."

"Then go in the back."

"It's dark back there. I'm afraid of the dark."

John heard a muffled cry, a scream between tightly sealed lips. "What are they doing?"

Frank stared straight ahead. "They're learning The Rest of the Story."

"That's bad Frank," said Seal. "This is no time for jokes, Buddy. My sense of humor said 'so long' and I wanna follow it. Where's your pity?"

"It died with my career ten years ago when that fucking Russian joker in there decimated my team. Shut up." Frank held up a hand.

Pavlenko was speaking rapidly. They heard short questions, longer explanations. Occasionally, he might pause, then he would gasp, then speak again, rapidly.

"Seems our friend Volodya ..." said Frank. "Oh my."

"What?" It came from John and Seal at the same time.

"Volodya is a loose round, working for his old bosses only nominally. He's in—to the blood—with one of the biggies in the Russian mafia, one of the thieves under the code. He wants—they want—Semi-anov's list. A destabilized America is candy, too rich a plum to pass up. Think of the opportunities, the territories to be gained. Volodya asked Sergei for the list."

There was another strangled cry.

"Sergei would not tell him because...."

A long gasp.

"Because of the file that is with the list. He could not trust Volodya. Volodya would...." Frank shook his head. The talking behind them resumed.

"Volodya knows Mara is the key," translated Frank. "The teams are for her. To make Sergei give up the list."

Steve spoke. Frank translated. "Give him the goddammed list."

A gasp and more Russian from Pavlenko.

"No," said Frank. "Volodya resented Sergei's victory. He is the better intelligence officer, but it was Sergei who beat Sobieski. Give Maximovich the file and he will hunt her forever. If he catches her...."

The last Russian words were lost in a full scream.

John swerved, then centered the RV in its lane. His heart pounded.

"Does this happen often?" he asked Frank.

Seal answered, "Too often."

"More than zero is too often," said Frank.

"Because it's evil?" said John.

Seal furled his forehead. "Because it's useless. There are easier ways. But they're not as satisfying."

Frank continued to translate as more Russian words came through the curtain like spurting blood. "What else is in the file?" "Nothing." "What else?" "Nothing." "What else?" "Oh God." A pause. "The location… and… layout of… Vasily's Carpet."

Seal and Frank looked at each other. "Holy shit!"

Frank held up his hand. "He got it from a servant. No! He infiltrated a servant."

"Brilliant!" said Seal. "The man's a genius. Too bad he's about to die."

Frank held up his hand again. "The asshole wrote it down!"

John did not think he could listen to any more of these strangled screams. There was no more talking after this one.

"He's dry," said Frank.

"What is Vasily's Carpet?" asked John.

"Their den, their lair, the place where they like to think they're safe, where they lock up their women and other valuables. Blown. By one bright Russian with an overactive pen. The disaster is enormous. This is worse than ten years ago."

A hand reached through the curtain and jerked Seal backward by the shirt collar. Steve's head poked through. "Pull over," he told John.

John pulled into a scenic stop overlooking a valley of rocks. There were several other cars there, and people with cameras. There was no green van.

"Seal's driving," Steve told Frank. "Get on the phone and grease things. We left all our brass back there."

He looked at John and said, "You come with me."

TWENTY-EIGHT

J ohn followed Steve, groping in the gloom between the bunks, and sensed a body in the lower right-hand bunk. It groaned and moved.

Steve handed him a flashlight.

"He's not beaten up this time," said John.

"That was revenge. This is business. Ask him which one he prefers."

The patient seemed untouched, except for the eyes. They were older. They did not belong in the face of a man in his thirties. John moved his clothing aside and came across the marks, most of them burns, in places that made him shudder.

"This is grotesque," he said.

"No shit," said Steve.

"I mean the whole thing. Everything. The fear, the hunger, the filth, the violence."

"So do I."

John dabbed at a burn with some useless ointment, trying to decide if it would need a dressing. It was an electrical burn. Most of the damage would be under the surface.

"She saved my life," said the patient. He grabbed John's arm. "The Frenchman pulled my head back by the hair, stretching my neck. Mack put his knife here." He pointed at his esophagus. "She put her hand on his hand. He stopped. I am alive. When it began, I knew I would die. When they put the iron there," he pointed to his crotch, "I wanted to die. I had to say it all before death. But, I am alive. Donovan never said anything when we did it to him. But we were enemies, and I did not hold it there that long!"

"You held it twice as long, you son of a bitch." Steve slipped a small bottle into John's hand as he said this.

It was morphine. John drew up the dose.

"God bless you, Doctor," Pavlenko said when he saw the needle. "It was not something she should see."

He drifted off so rapidly that John had a sudden fear that this was some silent form of murder, but he checked the vitals, and all was well. The patient rested.

John stood and faced Steve. "I can take her out of here, out of this."

"I wish you could."

"I have the money, the connections."

Steve frowned and shook his head slowly. "You don't have the intelligence—and I don't mean you're stupid."

...

If John thought their one sane exchange meant a change for the future, he was wrong. Steve pulled him off his bunk as usual four hours later. On this occasion, though, John woke quickly. On his way to the floor, he found time to pull his knee up, pushing it into Steve's kidney. Steve grunted, picked him up, and threw him backward toward the door. John landed at Mack's feet. Louis stood behind Mack, his hand holding the supporting strap of the top left bunk.

Louis chuckled.

"He kicked me in the back," said Steve. "But it didn't hurt."

"You saw him," said John to Mack. "Hit him. He was fighting and fair is fair."

Louis laughed out loud. "Do you remember, Misha, when you were given that new football? How I wanted it! You were only eight and you hit me so hard when I took it."

"I was seven. You were eight, and you fought dirty."

"And all the nannies screamed '*Lieber Gott*, they will kill each other!'"

"And Frau Giesel tried to box your ear. You bit her hand."

"You did that, Misha. I was wrongly accused. But then your father came to stop it. His solution was perfect."

Misha nodded. "We never fought again."

"Until Alex."

"Until Alex." Mack looked down at John on the floor. "I wish I could tie them together for a day, leg to leg, arm to arm." To Steve, who looked more than a little foolish, he said, "Go, sleep."

Louis dragged the doctor to his feet and led him forward.

John grumbled about the injustice until he met Mara in the galley and pulled her close to him. He was feeling irresistible.

"No more, John," she said.

"How can I have more when I haven't had any?" He tried again.

"I said no!" She pulled away and gave a questioning look to Louis. "Like that?" she asked.

Louis nodded.

"Do you think it will work?"

He shrugged.

John watched her walk to the back, heard the words "No more, Steve," and took a step to follow her, but Louis pulled him through the galley and sat him down at the table.

The patient was awake and sitting across from him, looking no more uncomfortable than the rest of them. He wore the headphones attached to the tape machine.

"Hey!" John said to Louis. "How come you trust him and not me?"

"We know him. We know him well. We do not know you at all."

Frank drove, with Mack as passenger. The chess set was out, and John played chess with Sergei. On the fourth move, Sergei leaned over the board and said, "I have taken your queen and my next move is mate."

John launched himself over the table, aiming for the man's throat. Sergei was weakened by his bruises and burns, so the match was almost even, with Sergei slowly winning.

Mack came out of the cab and helped Louis pull them apart.

"I'm okay. I'll stop." John puffed the words and shook himself.

"So much for your Hippocratic oath," said Mack.

John could still feel shame. It was an emotion among many others that crowded in a thronging queue. He slumped into the seat across from Sergei. "I'm sorry," he told him. "I thought you were saying something else."

Sergei's yellow, blue, and green face began a slow smile, partly hidden under the brown stubble, that told John he had not made a mistake.

John clenched his fist. "I'm just so tired," he said. "And I'm so fucking hungry!"

"So eat," said Louis.

"Eat what? There's no food!"

"Who told you that?"

"Who told me that?" John tried to remember. "Frank told me."

Louis laughed.

Frank's voice came from behind the curtain. "Uh, I meant to tell you the truth later, Doc. It slipped my mind. Sorry."

Louis opened the cabinet beside the refrigerator, a cabinet John only now noticed. He took out a flattened black plastic pouch and threw it at John. It was labeled, "Meal, ready to eat."

John was ready. He ate.

Mack poured two cups of coffee at the sink. "For a minute, I thought you were becoming one of us, Doctor. But a true spook verifies everything he is told. He also knows the entire contents of his environment. That is how I knew Jay had good information about you being a brilliant surgeon. No one can fake such a complete lack of training."

"If I'm so harmless, why was I under guard when you went over the ridge back there?"

Mack smiled a rare smile. "If success comes from brilliance, disaster comes from idiocy. Even geniuses have their moments of supreme stupidity. Do they not, Sergei?"

The Russian dropped his eyes.

"You have had more than a few such moments here, Doctor. Please do not be offended if I lock you out of my operating room. I did not say you are harmless. You lack only training and enemies. Everything else is there. But overall, you are what we call dead weight."

...

You would think that dead weight would be allowed to sleep, John thought, as he crawled into the passenger seat of the cab. He was told to stay up through the next shift. Steve was driving.

"Do you think this is their way of tying us together?" he asked Steve when they were back on the highway.

"Get us some coffee."

"I don't think I can drink anymore. The toilet's full again."

"Then get *me* some coffee, asshole."

"I didn't realize we were so close to El Paso," John said when he came back with the coffee. "Frank said you're from Texas. Is that right?"

No answer.

John stared at the blackness outside, the rush of the tarmac under the RV's headlights, the flash of a reflective mile marker.

He tried again. "And Seal is from Texas, too," he said. "And you were both babysitters. I thought Seal was in counterintelligence. That's what he told me, but Frank said he's a babysitter."

"He is in CI, but he was trained as a babysitter."

John tasted relief at the sound of Steve's voice. Keep him awake, Louis had said, or I will add more color to your face. *Whatever happened to simple requests?*

"So why did he leave?"

"He was forced out. There's an unwritten rule in the babysitter business. Killers are dirty; they contaminate. Babysitters hide their consciences behind the fact that they don't pull the trigger. Some even get the idea that their only job is to protect innocents. They take it all too literally, and if you kill on an operation, they give you a hard time."

"And Seal killed?"

"No. I mean, yes, he has killed. He was a SEAL in Southeast Asia."

"The Navy commandos? Seal was a commando?"

"Yeah. He's put on some weight."

"Some!"

Steve drained his cup, held it out to John.

John brought back more coffee.

"Seal didn't kill as a babysitter," Steve resumed. "That was the problem. He took all that shit seriously. He didn't pull the trigger when he should have, and he lost his team."

"Lost them?"

"Dead. Seven men dead, the mission a failure, sixteen hostages killed. It should not have been the end of his career, but he never got over it. Frank told me about it after my first op—in Chicago—because I did pull the trigger. A tango was about to shoot Charlie. I already knew all about what a crock of shit an official order can be, so I didn't have any problem making my decision. But they made my life hell in The Section after that."

"You became a specialist then?"

"No." He took a long sip of coffee.

John found himself thinking, reminded himself thinking could be dangerous. "What, exactly, would you say makes a specialist, Steve?"

Steve sipped his coffee again, adjusted his shoulders, and shifted his hands on the wheel. He glanced at John as he did this, sizing up the questioner with the question.

"First," he said finally, "is skill. Corollaries to that are work, training, experience, and above all, judgment. There are no substitutes." He paused as they passed a car ahead of them. "Second, of course, a specialist has to be able to pull a trigger, or whatever. Able in the sense of having the will, not just the skill."

"Does it ever bother you? Do you have nightmares about people you've killed?"

"Shit, no. My nightmare is getting shot in the face before I can shoot back. It doesn't bother me to kill the reptiles we go up against."

"Mack said enemies make a specialist."

"Yeah. I guess that's the third ingredient. It takes all our energy to stay one step ahead of them, and it takes money, information, and guns."

"How do you get enemies like that?"

John watched Steve as he asked this question. He saw the momentary expression of pain as Steve closed his eyes and set his jaw forward. He did not answer right away. When he did, he spoke with a quiet, tired voice.

"You know, John, I could kill you easily. It wouldn't take much to do it, and it wouldn't take much to make me do it. Say you whispered in Mara's ear, or touched her cheek, in front of me, with nobody else around to stop me, and say I was tired and strung out on adrenaline and under constant operational pressure at the time, like I am now. Then I'd probably kill you without thinking about it much, but it would be a fucking mistake, you might say—you, especially, might say—an atrocity, unjustified for any reason. Say you had powerful friends and family who might want justice. Those are the worst enemies, the ones who have a good reason for revenge and the means to carry it out."

"Mara can't have any of those."

"She has all of ours, the kind that wants us dead for good reason and the bastards that don't need a reason. She's a tool, a way to get at us, a way to get us. Now that she's operational, she'll gather her own set, the first ones being the two-bit slugs in every corner of the world who want to make a name for themselves by killing a specialist named Sobieski.

"Right now, that name is a more potent poison than the genetic link to Misha, in every sense, because it's as Vasily's daughter that she is most important to us. He was dead before I joined the team, but I'm always hearing, 'Mara's stubborn, just like Vasily,' or 'Mara fights like Vasily,' or 'Doesn't Mara smile like Vasily?'

"Isn't that the guy Pavelenko said he helped kill?" John searched his waning memory of the past few hours.

Steve nodded. "It was his life ambition to parole Mara from Vasily's Carpet. We managed to send her to a girl's college for two years, got her that job on the fringes of the game, and arranged for Seal to babysit. Now she's operational." Steve shrugged.

"You mean she has killed somebody? On the ridge back there?"

Steve did not answer him.

"And do you have enemies like that, Steve? Just because you shot one guy in Chicago?"

"No." He glanced at John. "I flew F-15s for the Air Force before I was a babysitter. Do you remember the airliner shot down over the Bering Sea twelve years ago?"

"Yes. Was that you?"

Steve nodded. "It wouldn't be so bad if somebody who lost his family on that airplane came after just me. I could call it justice and almost mean it. But there are half a dozen contracts out on my ex-wife and my son. My ex is an airhead, John. She doesn't know what an F-15 looks like, even after years of looking at the fucking model I kept on my desk. My son was born during the court-martial. If I die tomorrow, the contracts stay in force. So did Sobieski's, by the way, but by the time Mara went to college, most of them had been forgotten."

"But Mack?"

"There, you're catching on," said Steve. "Misha could walk up to his worst enemies right now and offer his body to science and they'd still want Alex. They'd cut her throat over his grave, just to say, 'So there.' Misha's not a good parent for Mara to have publicly. And his enemies don't forget. We're talking centuries here, as I understand it."

"Why do you call it Vasily's Carpet?"

Steve shifted in his seat, impatient. "Sobieski bought a rug in Beirut and put it in the hallway, to make it seem less like a prison. He hated prison. But at least it was safe. Now it's not." He turned on the turn signal. "There's a rest stop up here. Punch up the stop and turn on the sensors. I have to go."

"Hurry up," said Louis from behind the curtain. "We are next."

They pulled into the RV side of the rest stop. The taillights of a car disappeared up the ramp onto the highway. Otherwise, there was no traffic, not even a semi. It was about two in the morning.

John and Steve headed for the men's room on the right. They walked over the Lone Star embedded in the pavement and entered the building from the truck side. Steve checked the parking lot on the other side. There were no cars there.

John could smell it as soon as he came around the stone wall and faced the wall of sinks. He knew the smell now. Cordite. Steve knew it, too, and slammed him against the wall on their left, slammed himself against the opposite wall, and drew his Beretta. They rounded the corner cautiously. There were three stalls. The first was empty. The second was open; the door creaked slightly. Something sticky oozed toward the floor drain. John knew this smell, too.

Steve checked the third stall, empty, and came back to the second. He pushed the door open wide. Roger sat on the commode, in a suit and tie, with a neat hole in his forehead. John tried not to step in the blood as he took the wrist. He looked at Steve. "He's dead," he said.

"Shit, John, I'm fucking glad you went to medical school so you could give me that dipshit diagnosis. How about we get the fuck outta here."

TWENTY-NINE

Seal tried clearing his throat, then waving, then shouting. Finally, he jumped up and down. This cost him because he had to go as bad as the rest of them, but it was the only way. When at last they turned toward him, he pointed to the tape.

Charlie told him to turn on the external speaker.

"But why didn't Roger tell me this?" said Judy over the wire.

"I told you he said he'll meet us in San Antonio." It was Jane Jared's voice.

"I, um, we are supposed to.... I can drop you off in Fort Stockton, Jane, but I...."

"Roger told me all about what you're doing, Judy. He asked me to help you since he can't be here. It was an unexpected lead, he said."

"But he didn't explain it?"

"No. Now you get some sleep. I'll wake you up in two hours."

...

The doc was driving., with Steve in the passenger seat. Seal leaned over the sink staring vacantly at Mara's back in front of him. Charlie brought the cell phone down from the comm bank and sat on the booth seat across from Mara. He called Jay Turner, told him Roger was dead, and asked for the carphone number in Roger's car.

Seal made himself as small as possible—would have crawled up into the faucet given enough magic —and listened as the tape turned to the sound of the ringing phone.

"Hello," said Jane.

"Is it Roger?" said Judy.

"Shhh!"

"Hi," said Charlie.

Seal was hearing both sides of the conversation. Charlie must know that. Something made Seal not want to draw attention to it, even though he had an urge to run and get Frank.

Jane paused before answering, "Michael," with no hint of surprise.

"Who's Michael? Ow! You don't have to hit me," said Judy.

"How did you know where to find me?" Jane asked.

Steve poked his head through the curtain. "Oh Shit," he mouthed silently.

Charlie waved him away. "I was there, Jane," he said into the phone.

With a straight face.

Another pause. "Then why didn't you save the poor schmuck?"

"What schmuck? Ow! All right. Stop hitting." Judy harrumphed and fell silent.

"Was it your first?" asked Charlie.

"No."

"Who gave the order?"

"You know who."

"Why?"

Silence.

"Have you been given the order for me?"

More silence.

"So is he a boyfriend? He had his hands all over you when you met that team with the white van."

"You can't be jealous. You promised, remember, no promises."

"I lied."

Jane laughed. It was a beautiful deep, merry laugh.

"He's like a pimp, Michael. I imagine your babysitters treat you that way."

"Not quite."

"Well, they will treat Mara that way."

Charlie looked up at Seal, who stopped mid-chew on a piece of pound cake, his gray-stubbled chin dusted with crumbs.

"I doubt it," said Charlie.

"This is the pits," said Jane. "I'm sorry."

"You don't have to be. Come to me."

"I can't. They own me."

"I'll buy you."

Another rumbling laugh, like an earthquake.

"Yassuh, Massuh!"

"You brought it up. You said they own you. Let them name their price."

"And our brown-eyed babies will be the scandal of your family."

"My family can handle it."

"You think so, Romeo? You come to me."

"I can't."

"Why?"

"You know I would not survive, and besides, your side is wrong."

"Oh, I see. I'm the one who has to change. I have to give up everything I've ever known, everything I've ever believed, to be your ornament, to be quasi-accepted by your people. Is that it, Michael? And why? Because you have a corner on the truth? What if my side is right?" Her voice had come up a note.

"It isn't. We are running out of time to argue, Janie. Meet me somewhere."

"I don't know what your procedures are, Michael, but if they're anything like ours, I don't want to do that. I don't want to spend months in a black hole having my brain vacuumed, not even for you my darling, not even for you. I'd go mad without sunlight. And after that, then what? Where do you guys lock up your women? Do you know how badly Volodya wants your sister? He foams at the mouth. He's rabid with Mara disease. Do you want to saddle me with an army of enemies like Volodya? My life is shitty, Michael, but yours is shittier."

Charlie's forehead rested on his left hand. His right hand held the phone to his ear. He paused long enough to stop the tape through silence.

"Goodbye, my darling," she said as she put the phone down.

"Why are you crying?" asked Judy.

Mara reached across the table and took Charlie's hand. He gave her a half smile and stared at the phone. He drew circles around it with his index finger.

The tape ran again, briefly.

"Shit," said Jane. "I should have said I'd meet him and got it over with. But I can still use it later. He'll come. God, that's low."

"What's low?" asked Judy.

"Did you ever prosecute somebody you were pretty sure didn't do the crime?"

"Sure."

"So he went to jail?"

"She. Yep."

"And you don't feel bad about it?"

"Why should I? I won."

"But how is that justice, if somebody else did it and is still free?"

"She probably did other things, would have done more. She was the type—and anyway, I won."

"Winning is all there is?"

"You got it."

"Thanks, Judy."

Seal wanted to say something about this conversation, but the RV was pulling over. He marked the place with cellophane tape and rushed to the first available bush. By the time he was empty, so was his head. Steve and the doc were back in the RV and Charlie and Mara had taken the car down the road to get fuel. Steve handled the radio link to the car. Seal and the doc found a deck of cards and played War.

After twenty minutes, Charlie's voice came over the radio. "This is not good."

"Shit," said Steve.

"What?" said the doctor.

Steve was pulling open the footlocker in the corner, telling the doctor to get his blinking blank over here and help by blinky blank. He handed the doc a Texas license plate, a screwdriver, and strips of red vinyl trim.

"He only said something isn't good," said John.

"It's one of the ways we practice radio discipline. The more understated the words, the worse the situation. You switch the back plate and put this trim over the wheel wells. I'll do the front. Seal, wake the others and watch the sensors."

In twenty minutes, after the RV had been transformed, they heard, "… on our way."

Mack and Louis were putting on their gear and were almost dressed when the fireball went up in a

field about a mile away. They told Steve to stay behind and were out the door before the second explosion sent another red and gold plume into the night.
Steve pointed his MP5 at everybody.

"Did you hear that?" Judy said in Seal's ear.

The infrared sensors picked them up on their way
back ten minutes later. There were four figures on the
screen, the smallest glowing brighter than the rest.
Steve took no chances, covering the door even after all
recognition signals had passed.

The first one in was Mara, propelled by her
brother behind her. Then came the two older men.
The cordite smell was nothing new to Seal, but he noticed the doctor wrinkle his nose at it. There was another smell, too, that Seal could not place. It took a
minute for the confusion to resolve itself, on orders
from Mack. He was sent to the wheel, Frank to the
phone, Sergei to the radio to monitor the police nets.
Charlie gave a quick and dirty in German. Everybody
turned to the doctor. Seal paused on his way to the
cab and saw Mara turn around. He saw the doctor's
face as he looked at the glistening, muddy burns
down one side of her back.

Shoved into the driver's seat, Seal started the engine and put the truck into gear. He heard Mara's
cool, slow voice behind him, telling the doctor, "There
were cows in the field. The manure put the fire out
quickly. I was lucky. Don't you think so?"

THIRTY

John began cutting. He reached out his left hand for the box of morphine. Charlie snatched it away. John dropped the scissors and lunged after it. Louis turned him around and put the scissors back in his hand. "Not yet," he said. "She must stay alert."

"But it's filthy. The wounds are filthy. I'm going to have to get all of that out."

Steve sat next to her on the bench, his arm around her hips. "You shouldn't wear that chain, Mara."

"It won't garrote me. It will break easily. My father gave it to me. It's lucky."

"*Wie Vasily*," Mack mumbled. He tore open another package of gauze and arranged it on the table with the others.

John gave her a solid dose of antibiotics, then finished cutting away her shirt and jog bra, his stomach turning at the sight of blistered and bleeding wounds covered in manure. Sergei unbuckled her holster and took it off her carefully.

Charlie brought a bottle of good scotch out of the coffee cabinet. He poured some into a Styrofoam coffee cup and handed it to Mara.

"She needs water now, not alcohol. It's dehydrating," said John. They all stared at him, appalled. *I know I'm right.* "Besides," he said aloud. "You said she has to stay alert."

"This much will not impair her," said Charlie. "And it is not the same as a drug." He began pouring scotch into more Styrofoam cups until everybody had one. He offered one to John.

John watched Mara as she drank it, matched her in tossing it down. It warmed him inside, reminding him that he had an inside, a welcome internal warmth that made the outside heat more bearable. Charlie was right. It was not a drug. It was a gift.

Sergei found a more or less clean tarpaulin in the shower and spread it on the littered floor. Mara lay on this, face down, her arms stretched out over her head. Louis lay along her arms so that his long legs touched the GPS in the cab. He held her shoulders, his head next to hers. He spoke to her quietly in French. Steve held her legs. Sergei relayed clean bandages from the table to John's outstretched hand.

John worked quickly, ruthlessly, to get the manure out of the raw wounds on her back. A splash of burning fuel had formed a mark that snaked down the right side from shoulder to waist. John pulled bits of clothing out of a charred hole, a piece of leather from the cross strap of her holster from another wound near the waist, and two small stones out of another gash, higher up. He cleaned and disinfected, killing every nest of bacteria there could be, he hoped. Then, he disinfected again. He laid on the burn oint-ment, then the anesthetic ointment, since that would not make her groggy, and he checked her vitals for signs of shock. There were none. She had not made a sound.

The men all turned away while he helped her sit up and wrapped her chest to hold the dressings. Charlie gave her a clean black T-shirt. Dressed and alert, she sat at the table, careful not to lean back against the booth, and demanded more scotch.

"John says you need water first," said Steve.

Sergei handed her an eight-ounce bottle of miner-al water, cold from the refrigerator.

She stuck her tongue out at it. Charlie pointed at the water, and she drank it.

"You do the briefing," he told her as he poured more scotch into her cup. He put both babysitters in the cab and gave John the headphones. John had no idea what he was supposed to listen for but stood be-hind the sink feeling triumphant at this new expres-sion of trust. The team began stripping and cleaning weapons, as usual. Charlie refilled the magazines for his and Mara's Glocks. Mara sipped her scotch and gave her briefing.

"When I came out of the bathroom," she said. "I saw nothing, but I felt something. I made eye contact with Charlie, who was at the pumps, and could see he felt it, too. There seemed no basis for it, though, so I went inside to pay for the gas.

"I was third in line at the counter. The line stretched across a crossway aisle and down a center aisle to the door. I edged to the left, near shelves of canned goods, to be closer to cover and also to use the surveillance mirrors in the far corners. There were other people in the shop, two women to the right at the soda machine, a man at the back looking at magazines, plus the two men in front of me in line.

"I saw them before they came through the door. No one in the shop was moving wrongly, so I concluded that everything would come from outside and kept watch there. I crouched closer to the canned goods and drew my weapon. I had already chambered a round. I was open on three sides, but there was nothing I could do about it without cutting off my escape.

"They came in four abreast, but the first three were quickly telescoped behind one another because of the narrow aisle. They carried Uzis. I decided this was not a robbery. The first one fired a controlled burst at the ceiling and shouted for everyone to get down. I do not think they expected me to be right in front of them because they were looking at the mirrors to see down the aisles.

"I am sure I hit the first man in the chest, but he must have worn soft body armor. He did not go down. I stood up and stepped partly behind the shelving, now on my right since I was facing the door. On the next round, I used a silhouette point at the head, and he went down. I knew the one behind him would be similar, adjusted the silhouette for his head (he was slightly shorter) and he went down.

"I did not think I had time for the third, as his muzzle was already bearing on me and his weapon was in full automatic, clearing the shelves to my left. Besides, I could see that Charlie was at the door, trying to acquire the target and I was in the way. I ducked behind the shelving to my right, thinking to use the right-hand aisle to approach the door. I was quickly surprised by the fourth man, who was also surprised. We almost collided, and so neither of us had a chance to bring our weapons to bear. I used the opportunity to try to knock the Uzi out of his hands with an outside crescent kick. I was not successful. He was quite large. I needed height and power and so I chose a tornado kick to the head. He fell back into a display of soft drink cans, but I do not think he was dead. I met Charlie at the door."

"This took?" asked Mack.

"Three, perhaps four seconds," she replied.

He looked at Charlie. "Did you get the third man?"

"Yes."

"We assumed there would be two more outside," Mara continued, "because we had accounted for four and Sergei said that Maximovich uses teams of six.

We were correct. We covered each other to the car, but the windshield was blown out on our way to the highway."

"We did not have time to reinforce the glass in Reno," explained Louis.

Mara shrugged, then winced. Her face had turned a vivid crimson in the heat. John stepped over half a dozen gun parts and cleaning rods to get to her. Her pulse was steady, though, and she was not finished.

"Charlie drove," she said, "and I tried to read the map. The two remaining men pursued us in a dark-colored van. When the rear window of our car blew out, Charlie ducked, then swerved to avoid a slower car. We left the road and traveled through a barbed wire fence into a rocky pasture. A rock must have punctured one of the tanks because we began to smell gasoline rather strongly. Charlie told me to get out. I obeyed."

She paused for approval. Everyone nodded. Good girl.

"I landed in manure," she continued. "And the car traveled to the right so that it almost circled me before it stopped. This is why I was not far enough away when the first tank exploded. I rolled in the manure, and when the fire was out, I ran toward a ditch a hundred meters away on my left. I was in the ditch by the time the second tank went up.

"I heard Charlie's call and I answered. He found me in the ditch. We were deciding our location when we heard your call and we replied."

THIRTY-ONE

I t fell to John's shift to solve the fuel problem.

"We have to turn on the air conditioner," John told Louis. "It must be a hundred degrees back there. Mara will be in agony." He sat in the passenger seat sipping his coffee and adjusted the air vent. It was already hot, and the sun was not yet up.

The dawn put lights and shadows on Louis's face as he drove the RV. It made him look more sinister than usual, which was considerable. His dark hair had long since slipped its bonds and its curls waved over his head in gray-flecked excursions. His beard was thick, coarse, and matted. He had a look in those almost-black eyes that would make any sensible person cross a street to avoid him.

John liked him the best of them all. Louis's jokes were usually crude but always funny. He was mercurial and violent but devoted to Mara.

"We must conserve the petrol," Louis said. "Until Misha decides the safest way to get more. Mara suffers now no more than a man would. She is all right."

"What? No more than a man?"

Louis then casually turned the switch on the back air conditioner to high. This was another thing John liked about him. You could never tell what he was thinking simply by listening to what he was saying.

Louis drank his coffee and glanced at the road once or twice while he watched John. "My Uncle Bertrand taught me from the time when I was eight years old," he explained. "He taught me to fight, to kill, to listen. These are important skills. He also told me about women. He told me all the ordinary things that boys learn, but the training he gave me was more than what is considered ordinary. He also taught me about the women in this business.

"Uncle Bertrand explained it is theoretically possible for a woman to be as effective as a man of her weight. He said with good training, a woman could be formidable in her class. We have now proved this with Mara.

"But, my uncle insisted, a woman is most effective when she is allowed to be herself. Use her for honey traps, he said. When she kills, she should do it with finesse, not strength, because she has more of the one than the other. She is subtle. This is her advantage.

"It also can be her disadvantage. When she suffers ordinary hardship and pain, she suffers them the same as any man, according to her strength. But add intelligence to the pain, let it target the soul, and here she differs. A man's response will be physical. He will be too angry or too busy to appreciate a subtle torture, but a woman will grasp its full impact.

"This is why, Uncle Bertrand insisted, while you may use a woman, or you may marry a woman, never have one on your team. If she is ever made to suffer as a woman, you will not be able to bear it. This is what I mean when I say that, for now, Mara suffers as a man."

John stared at him. "*You* will not bear it?"

"I will not. We will not. The men will not. Cannot. The relationships within the team are … I am at a loss." Louis looked at the road for half a mile, searching for English words written in the lane lines.

"During great stress," he continued finally, "the bonds between us are more important than all of the training and all of the equipment. We think, move, act, and suffer together. If we cannot, then there is no bond, or it is a foreign bond. In any case, it is useless under the conditions we face."

"Then what will you do about Mara?" asked John, incredulous.

"Do?" Louis raised an eyebrow. "Nothing. Wait for Mara to see it. It has been explained to her, but she does not know it. Some wisdom comes with maturity. We hope she hurries."

"But the risks?"

"There are always risks in bringing up children."

Mack spoke up from behind the curtain.

"Take this exit."

Louis parked the RV on a side road behind a few mesquite trees. Misha and Frank explained the plan for the shift.

"We will clean up the doctor," said Frank.

"Because he smells," said Sergei.

"So do you," said John.

"Get him a fresh shirt and jeans," said Frank, "and an electric razor."

John kicked Sergei. Sergei kicked back.

"Please." Frank exaggerated the word, spreading his lips like a chimpanzee.

With prodding, John stripped and dressed in the middle of the room and listened to his briefing while he buttoned on a starched blue and red striped shirt. He took it off again so he could shave without getting his beard all over it.

"There is a large truck stop about five miles further along the highway," said Mack. He pointed to the computer screen. Sure enough, there it was. "The vehicle is disguised. You are the least well-known of us all. The watchers will be looking for at least two people in the cab, and someone to watch the payer's back. They will expect the person at the pump and the person paying to be in the same condition that Charlie and Mara were in at the last stop, that is, dirty and tired.

"You will go in looking fresh and alert and completely alone. We will turn on the cameras and sensors, but we will be very quiet. We will give you three minutes to pay. After that, we will leave without you. We cannot risk staying longer." He looked at Louis. "In that event, we must assume that Sergei is blown."

"It does not matter," said Louis. "Charlie wants to jettison all the dead weight."

"All?" asked Mack. "Who else does he include as dead weight?"

"Sergei and Seal."

"Seal is not dead weight. He is a master of trade-craft. Charlie would profit from lessons from Seal. Also, Seal is guaranteed to put himself between Mara and any bullet. I will speak to Charlie."

John held the razor an inch from his chin, waiting for the rest of this 'dead weight' discussion to clear up. It didn't.

He cleared his throat. "There can't be that many bad guys out there, can there? And how can they find us at one particular truck stop?"

The four men at the table stared at him. Frank answered finally. "Doc, the FBI, or at least some part of the FBI, is unwittingly helping the bad guys. There are lots of them."

"But they killed Roger and he was FBI." John's voice vibrated with the razor on his jaw.

"Jay Turner runs his own game, too, you know, and if Roger was one of his, and if the bad guys as you call them found out, well, then Roger's dance card would naturally be canceled. As for them finding us in one truck stop, they will be looking for us in all truck stops. They know we're on wheels. They know we blew up a whole car full of gas, and they can put two and two together, come up with four, and put that many watchers at every station between here and San Antonio."

John finished shaving one side of his face and began on the other, gently over the bruises. "What do I do if they catch me? Will they shoot me, do you think?"

Mack shook his head.

"Tell them that Sergei is with us, and your FBI should guarantee your safety. Tell it to them, not to Maximovich. If he catches you, tell him you will talk only to the FBI."

Sergei shook his head. "It will not help. Don't you see, Mack, the only way you can jettison the doctor is to shoot him? John has spent more than two days with you. He knows your habits, attitudes, and working relationships. Everybody talks too much. He knows that Frank is forgiven, that Charlie finally made Mara obey him, and that you might give quarter, but Charlie never will. He knows Steve is in a lather over Mara, and Louis would march into hell for her. Volodya will ream our good doctor until he gets it all."

Louis snorted. "For what?"

Sergei stared back at the Frenchman for a moment, deciding how to explain this. "Have you told me how you plan to get the file?" he asked.

"No," Mack answered.

"Then I will tell you your plan. Charlie and Steve will create a diversion by going into the warehouse through the roof. While they pin down Volodya's teams from above, Louis will open the lock on a side door. You will run point for him, taking them out silently with the knife. He will open the correct safe while you set a diversionary charge. That charge will also be a signal for Charlie and Steve to get out. They will secure one door. You will exit together."

Mack and Louis were silent.

Frank spoke. "You figured that out from listening to Charlie and Mara bicker?"

"Among other things," said Sergei. "When Sobieski was alive, the three of them worked as a single team. Now, they have become effectively two teams, with twice the coverage and the ability to create diversions. The watch system alone during this trip shows this. The point is, that to a brain like Volodya's, the doctor is vitamin-enriched protein. He is not dead weight."

Thank you, Sergei Pavlenko. John put the razor on the table and almost shook his hand.

"He is poison," said Louis. He pointed at Sergei. "And so are you."

"All medicine is poison," said Mack. He pointed at John. "Put your shirt on and start driving. And do not get caught."

THIRTY-TWO

They've solved it, thought Seal. He opened his eyes and watched Steve slide off the bunk above him. The room was cool, almost cold. They got the gas, thought Seal, and the air is on high. He wondered if Mara had slept at all.

The doctor stood by Mara's bunk. He looked spiffy, all cleaned up, in a striped shirt and new blue jeans. Steve took this opportunity to ram his shoulder into him on his way out. Shift change was a series of thumps and bumps and shushes as everybody tried to get out at once and the other watch tried to get in and the doctor tried to look at Mara's back without waking her up. There was a long-whispered relay of 'Mara stays back this shift. Frank and Sergei stay up.'

Charlie was dragging mega-gear up front. Seal groaned. The guy was all work. Seal had now been days without play and was ready for a minor goof-off. No go with Charlie. Normally, Seal would not think about a boss's opinion in a decision to kick back, but normally the boss was not such a... Seal wanted to think the word fucking, but he had cleaned up his language considerably around Mara. If you think it, you'll say it, he always said. So his boss this trip was a damned error-free killing machine half his age. He was no good time Charlie, not by any stretch. Seal sighed and pushed the f...ing—damned—locker full of submachine guns in front of him into the galley.

This would be their last shift. At the end of it, they would be in San Antonio. After that, it was a straight go to the end. None too soon, in Seal's book. For a last shift, it was exactly like all the others, gloriously unexciting. He liked it that way. No f...ing cockups, no funerals. Seal took his turn on the tape machine, listened to Judy's stupid whining, and wondered why Jane didn't shoot her right then.

He also took a turn at the wheel, with Charlie as his passenger. Seal could have lived happily ever after without trying to make conversation with Sasquatch here, but Charlie became surprisingly civil. He asked polite questions. Seal would have been almost comfortable if this new warmth didn't make yesterday's dead weight talk stand out even more. The thought of ever being on this guy's bad side gave Seal the willies.

For the second half of the shift, Frank and Steve drove while Charlie and Seal checked the ropes and knots. Charlie asked for Seal's opinion. Seal gave it, carefully and showed Charlie a better knot. *Always ask a sailor.*

Sergei sat at the table next to Seal, trying hard not to be too visible to Charlie. He failed. While Seal re-knotted the ropes, Charlie pulled a long roll of white paper from between two radios overhead. He unrolled it on the table. It was a drawn floor plan of the warehouse containing the file.

"Let's go over this," said Charlie.

Sergei nodded. If we must.

"It's ten meters to the roof?"

"To the ceiling. Semianov said there is an iron catwalk, mid-way between ceiling and floor, all the way around, and that it is five meters from the floor. This suggests the roof is ten meters."

"How many rows of crates?"

"He did not say."

"How many rows of safes?"

"He did not say. He said to count the rows from the south staircase that descends from the catwalk. Fourth row of safes, from south to north, sixteenth safe east. The combination is 29-16-5-0. Look in the second drawer, sixth compartment."

"What does the rest of this look like?" Charlie swept over a wide white space on the paper with his hand.

"*Ne zhnaiyu.* Semianov said it is a U.S. Government temporary archive. Documents are held for up to eight years. He put the files in with documents to be retired to another archive in 1999."

"And Maximovich has the warehouse?"

"I am sure he has. Semianov told four of us about the warehouse. He told only me the exact location to find the documents. Maximovich interrogated the other two."

"He assassinated the other two?"

"Yes." Sergei squirmed. There was not much room next to Seal for squirming.

Charlie stared at him across the table, that still, blue stare that x-rayed you with maximum radiation. Seal didn't blame Sergei for sweating.

"I know why he wants the file," said Charlie quietly. "I know his plans for an American destabilization, and I know his underground alliances. I know his resources and his procedures. I even know some of his motivations. I appreciate that the KGB, or what was once the KGB, must find new work. I wonder what your plans were?"

"My future was assured. I escaped the chopping block and was designated for a directorate within the new foreign intelligence service, the SVR. My past success, my pre-Bolshevik family name." Sergei shrugged.

"But Maximovich was getting the axe?"

"Yes."

"And when he asked for your help, you refused because of the danger to Mara."

"Yes."

Charlie paused. "It's still not enough. Jane said 'rabid.' She said Maximovich is rabid about Mara. This is a personal thing, certainly related to you, but also having to do with Mara. What have you done to Maximovich that makes him target her, Sergei Nickolaevich?"

It was a direct, unavoidable question. Confession time. Seal wanted to leave the confessional. Lightning can miss. Even a close brush with it will burn you.

Sergei swallowed.

I bet he's remembering that iron. Not something I'd forget.

"Last year," said Sergei, "Volodya went to the Congo for several months on an operation. While he was gone ..." Sergei cleared his throat. "While he was gone, Nadhezda asked me to help her with her black market work."

"Nadhezda is?"

"Was. Volodya's wife—what Americans call common law. They lived together. I think they planned to marry someday. While Volodya was gone, I helped her out at the flat, and one night, we celebrated something, a killing on the market, I don't know what, and with the vodka and her loneliness, and...." Sergei raised his eyebrows.

Charlie did not shift his gaze. "You seduced her."

Sergei shook his head and threw up his hands. "She seduced me! I was helpless, I swear it! But she died in childbirth in March. I could not deny it was my child. The little thing had no one else. But the baby died a few days later. I thought Volodya had forgiven me when he asked me for the file. He was civil, almost friendly. He was my friend. I had to tell him why I could not help him."

"*Sheisse*. Did you spell it out for him? The file, the plans to Vasily's Carpet?"

"No. Only that it could damage Mara."

Mara poured herself a cup of coffee behind them, not making a sound. Her hand shook as it held the cup. Her eyes had sunk into black circles in a dirty face. Medusa had a better hairstyle. The fire had burned the top of her braided knot so that clumps of hair hung down or stuck out on either side, no longer containable by a rubber band. Mara put her cup down and removed what was left of the rubber band. Six inches of singed hair fell to the floor. She looked at it and burst into tears.

Seal and Sergei were right there, consoling her with cluck clucks, trying to figure out how to pet her without touching the burns on her back. Charlie sat at the table and rolled his blue eyes to the ceiling.

"I can fix it," said Sergei. "I need a scissors. Where is the doctor's bag? I will fix it." He rootled through the doctor's bag, found the scissors, and began snipping.

"A comb. A comb will help."

Seal produced one from a back pocket. He rinsed it with hot coffee over the sink.

Sergei did an acceptable job. She looked adorable in their eyes, even with short hair, but she kept on crying, and they stood around helpless and distressed. She cried onto Sergei's shoulder. He held her as tightly as he could but for the bandages, and she shook with sobs.

Seal jerked his shoulders and shook his hands to loosen the tension in his arms. He looked at the ceiling, then returned Charlie's ironic stare. He remembered the big black bow. Charlie was right again.

Charlie smiled.

Seal shuddered. He hated this mind reading shit.

Mack was the next one to come forward, and this was the little scene that greeted him. Sergei tried to look nonchalant, as though he didn't know how the girl crying on his shoulder got there. When Mara realized Mack was behind her, she stepped away from Sergei, forced her arms to her sides, and stood there, hub-chub-lubbing with tears streaking mud down her face.

Seal would not have believed it if he had read it in a file. Mack took a handkerchief from his pocket, gave it to Mara, and gathered her into his arms. The real sobbing broke out now, and with it came wailing and protests and reassurances, all in German. This is the guy with the knife, Seal told himself. *I've seen this. I'm a dead man.*

Charlie produced his usual helpful cup of scotch. Problem solved. The sobs subsided. Louis came forward and asked what the problem was. Steve pulled the van into a thicket on a side road and demanded to know what was going on. Frank came with him looking concerned. The doctor showed up last, rubbed his eyes, and wanted to know what's up. Mara smiled and hub-lubbed and sipped her scotch. Then everybody complimented her haircut.

Mack sent Frank and Sergei to the back to sleep. He told Mara she could sleep, too, but she had already taken the headphones and was making herself busy with the coffee machine. Charlie handed her the holster with her Glock in it and told her to put it back on. She found a new cross strap in the open weapons locker and had no shortage of people helping her put it together.

The room was in chaos, with Jay calling them on the cellular, the meeting beginning, and the plan prescribed for a reconnaissance. Seal made himself invisible in a corner until he might be needed, but the doctor had no clue and managed to stand directly in everybody's path. This wasn't hard to do in such a tight space, but the doctor contrived to do it with spectacular results.

At one point, Steve fell past him, tripping over his feet, but was up on the rebound and coming straight at the poor schmuck with only one thing in mind. Seal was the closest man there, so he had no choice but to play punching bag. He bore Steve down with his weight mostly, and a minor resurrection of the skill he once had. Even so, Seal barely held him, and it took Charlie and Louis to pull Steve off and a sharp word from Mack to settle him into a slow seething.

The doc's jaw never came up off the floor. Somebody pushed him against the wall, and he stayed there, staring at the chaos, feeling the swell of violence as the adrenaline began that would carry them through a killing night. Seal gave him a pat on the shoulder, but he did not respond.

Mack and Louis were stripping and shaving and dressing in suits, with white shirts and ties, wires and transmitters, soft body armor and shoulder holsters, backup holsters with little .38s at the ankle, knives carried horizontally inside their belts and more of them tucked into scabbards carried in the crotch. Mack slipped a slim, light, sharp little number inside his tie.

Louis tamed his wild curls with mousse. Mack brought his hair under control with just water.

"Jay is meeting us at Dick's in someplace called the Riverwalk," Mack told Charlie. "He is bringing a car and says he has a safehouse for us. We will need fuel in the truck. Use the doctor. It worked well last time and might work again. At least it will keep them busy while we look at the warehouse. Then meet us in the parking lot by the bus station next to the Alamo. Here. I have marked it." He pointed at a map on the table.

The doctor asked a lot of stupid questions that nobody answered. Seal shoved him into the driver's seat and climbed into the seat next to him. He navigated them downtown and onto Crockett Street. They let Mack and Louis out a block away from Dick's.

"I'm supposed to be alone in the cab to get the gas," said the doctor. "They won't be looking for somebody alone."

"We want them to see us, Doc," Seal said in his most patient voice. "We want them to gather round."

"Do you know what they'll do to me if I get caught?"

"No. Do you?"

"I understand it's not pleasant."

"That's probably a safe assumption. Turn left at the next traffic light."

"But what should I do?"

Seal shrugged. "Don't get caught."

THIRTY-THREE

John could feel their eyes, their thoughts, their estimates. Two men with long hair and dirty white t-shirts edged closer to his pump. They were within twenty feet of him by the time the tank was full. He threw the nozzle back onto the pump and jogged to the shop.

The two men did not follow him.

He threw a fifty at the man behind the counter and said, "Keep the change."

"Hey! Is your name Jerry?" The man shouted over the heads of customers.

John was already at the door. He paused with his hand on the door rail.

"She said he'd be a blond guy in a hurry," said the man behind the counter, still shouting. "If you're Jerry, Jane says call her at the Merriot. Merriot Rivercenter."

John waved at him and ran to the RV. The truck was in motion before the door slammed shut behind him. Seal drove. Seal would lose the bums, Mara told him.

After John tumbled around inside for fifteen minutes, Steve handed him another license plate and a screwdriver and pushed him out the door again, into the staff lot of the city zoo. It was faster work this time. They tore off all the trim they had put on before, then tore off the previous trim underneath it. The RV now sported a set of slim purple lines and Louisiana plates.

John collapsed on the bench across from Charlie as they returned to the road. Charlie was cleaning his Glock.

"Any problems at the gas station?" he asked. He wet a cleaning pad with solvent.

John's brow wrinkled, puzzled. "The guy thought I was somebody named Jerry."

Charlie stopped and stared. "The exact words. I want the exact words."

Steve had two bags of gear and clothing on the floor by the time Charlie finished dialing the Merriot. He put the phone on speaker, so they could change their clothes while he spoke to her.

"I'm so scared, Michael," said Jane.

Mara closed one eye, thinking.

"Okay. Stay in your room," said Charlie. "I'll come to your room."

"It's Judy's room," said Jane.

"Not another fucking hotel room," mumbled Steve. He adjusted the Velcro at the shoulders of his soft body armor.

"Get Judy out of there," said Charlie.

"I can't. It's her room."

"I hate clearing a fucking hotel room," whispered Steve. He buttoned a white cotton shirt over the armor.

"Tell Judy how to act," said Charlie. "Tell her to keep her hands in view."

"Full of god-damned hidey holes and the first one's right behind the mother-fucking door." Steve pulled on a pair of summer weight brown wool trousers.

"I know," said Jane. "I'll tell her."

"I will put you in a safehouse. You'll be okay." Charlie reassembled the Glock as he spoke.

"And you fucking never, never know which fucking side the fucking son of a bitch bathroom is on." Steve slammed a full magazine back into his Beretta and slipped it into the holster under his arm.

"Tell Steve the bathroom is on the left side," said Jane. She sounded amused. "Hurry."

Click.

Charlie waved away the wire Mara offered. She frowned. "It'll scare her off," he said. "We don't need the wires. We'll clear the room and disarm them both. Steve will take Judy down to the lobby, slip away from her there, and meet us in the parking garage. We'll walk across, climb in the van, secure her gently, and be on our way."

He scowled at Mara's doubtful look. "It's on the next block, Mara, and utterly simple. We will not take chances."

She watched through the cab curtain until they were in the Rivercenter parking garage across the street.

John was elated. It was the first time since Reno that he found himself semi-alone with her. Seal was there, but that was all right. Seal didn't exploit every opportunity there was to hit him. John was not sorry Steve had to clear a hotel room, fucking or otherwise. He was not sure what clearing involved, but if Steve found it nasty, it made John smile to think of him doing it.

Mara was not smiling when she turned around. Her solemnity almost put a lid on his sudden high spirits, but he had to take his chance. Now.

She was looking past him with wide eyes. John took a step toward her, but turned around at the same time, to see what alarmed her. Seal stood in the galley, staring with the same wide-eyed expression at the tape machine. He reached toward the bottom reel, pulled a cellophane tab out with his fingernail. It had folded itself into the magnetic tape, and the conversation it marked had never been reviewed.

John would have liked to ignore it, except for the looks on Seal's and Mara's faces. Seal cued the tape and pressed play. While Mara listened to Jane say, "God, that's low," Seal brought a nylon bag up from the back.

"I'll need three magazines of subsonic hollow-point," she said. She pointed to the box of assorted guns and cartridges.

Seal began rummaging.

"And the suppressor. Mine is in the red case."

Seal pulled out a red case.

"Mara," said John.

"Not now, John."

"But ..."

"It's a trap, John. Jane is going to kill them. I have to go. I don't have time for other things right now."

"Go? You can't! It's dangerous."

She was already stripped to panties and bandages. Seal handed her a soft body armor vest and helped with the Velcro at the shoulders. She grimaced as the weight settled on her back. Next came a powder blue knit skirt. She buckled a web belt with loops and pockets over the waistband, picked up her Glock and inserted a full magazine, then practiced attaching a suppressor and returning it to its pocket. Finally, she chambered a round and slipped the Glock into the holster at her back. She drew it twice, practicing a smooth extraction. Seal handed her two more magazines. She put these into loops at the front. Seal put the earpiece of a wire into her left ear and arranged the wire down the front of her body armor. He plugged it into a box and clipped it to the belt. Before she put on an oversized loose knit top in powder blue to match the skirt, Mara slipped a small knife into an inner pocket in the breast of her body armor.

She sat on the folding chair to tie the straps of a pair of white string sandals. John wanted to reason with her.

"I know what I'm doing, John."

"I never said you didn't. I'm only suggesting that you should wait."

"Makeup, Seal. I need makeup. I look like hell."

Seal made up her face: eyeshadow, mascara, powder, blush, and lipstick, while she checked the draw on her Glock again, drew back the slide, and looked in the chamber.

"Don't move your eyes," said Seal. He brushed an eyelash gently. "I'll monitor the normal frequency. If Steve and Charlie come back, I'll tell you. What do I tell the other two if they come back?"

"Tell them the room number, 557. My plan is to warn and interrupt. That's all. Then, I will do as Charlie tells me. They can contact us on my wire. We will be here within ten minutes. I'm ready. How far ahead of me are they?"

"Six, maybe eight, minutes."

"I will make up time by running."

"I can't let you do this, Mara," said John. He blocked the door, determined, but only until Seal's three hundred pounds removed him. He was still trying to hit Seal when Sergei and Frank came out of the back room.

Seal threw him off and stood over the door. John sat on the floor holding his head in his hands.

"Where is Mara?" asked Pavlenko.

"Gone," John moaned.

"Jared set a trap for Charlie and Steve," said Seal. "She went to warn them."

"No!"

Sergei rushed the door, but Seal was prepared for this, repulsed him, and tackled him as he fell against the weapons locker. Frank stood looking stupid until Seal swore at him to move his ass and help, damn it. Frank pinned the Russian's arms so that when John tried to get up, Seal could send him sprawling again with a kick to the abdomen while he kept the bulk of his weight on Sergei's legs.

"Now listen up folks," said Seal as they lay in a twisted heap on the floor, "Mara is a specialist backing up a member of her team. There ain't shit we can do about it except support her as her babysitters. That means we stay here, keep this vehicle secure, and afterward, clean up any mess she makes. That's our job. That's our only fucking job. If you do anything else, you asshole Pavlenko, you'll put her in more danger. If you get yourself killed or caught, you'll put the whole fucking operation in jeopardy. I declare myself to be in charge—no offense Frank—and I expect my orders to be obeyed here. Is that clear, doctor?"

"Yes." He pulled his knees up and rolled onto them.

"Pavlenko?"

A grunt that could be taken either way.

John and Sergei climbed into the cab and stared out in the direction of the Merriot. Sergei should be undercover, Seal shouted from behind the curtain. "*Idi nakui*," came the reply. Frank kindly translated, "Go fuck yourself."

Sergei sat with his arms on top of the steering wheel and his chin on his hands. He and John were silent for a full ten minutes.

Then the sirens began.

THIRTY-FOUR

M ara hugged the wall to the right of the door labeled 557. Doors alternated on either side of
the narrow hallway. Mara chose the right side of the
door because a specialist leaving the room would be
oriented toward the emergency exit stairs on the left
instead of the elevators on the right.

There was no sign of Charlie or Steve, nor any
sound from the room. With her left fist, Mara pounded on the door. Nothing. She pounded again. She
heard movement. An older couple came out of their
room down the hall to the left, six meters away. The
door beside Mara opened; two bullets came through it
and into the opposite wall. The old couple was now
three meters away, with puzzled faces. The noise was
not excessive. The shooter had a suppressor. Jane ran
out of the room and into the old people. Her gun was
in her right hand. She wore a loose assortment of
flowing cotton in an African motif that wrapped itself
around the strap of the old woman's purse and set the
two innocents hollering for the police.

Jane took the woman's purse with her for almost
a meter before the cotton unraveled and let the purse
fall to the floor. The old man ran to pick it up while

his wife stood bawling and shouting in the middle of the hallway so that Mara still had the two of them between her and Jane. No unobstructed bead. Jane reached the door to the stairs.

Mara looked into 557, fearing the scene, but Charlie was up and about, more or less, tangled in bedclothes, but dressed and stumbling to the door, his Glock in his right hand. The suppressor was not on it. That meant the shots had been Jane's, random, to clear her egress. How careless Mara thought. She downgraded her estimate of Jane's abilities.

Mara decided that Charlie could fend for himself, and Jane would try for Steve next, in the lobby. She ran after her, knocking the purse out of the old man's hand as he tried to pick it up. She did not wait to see the blood on Charlie's hand or the hole in his coat. She did not hear him wheezing. The old couple did, though. They saw a blond man come out of that room, with blood on his left hand, a gun in his right, and his breath sounding like a bellows in a forge. The old man told this to the police later. The woman fainted.

The lobby was decorated for coolness in a hot climate, with refrigerated air, tile floors, and southwestern colors. It was crowded with rough-hewn furniture and too many plants. Plants that concealed without providing cover.

Mara arrived to find Jane poking her gun through a fern.

"Steve!" She raised her Glock, using a geometric point. A woman in spandex with a big purse and sunglasses stood screaming in front of a chair two meters from Jane.

"Ah! Ahhhh!" She waved her arms over her head, centering herself in Mara's sights.

Mara moved to the right. Jane fired and moved to avoid the return. Her movement brought her around the plant in plain sight of Steve, whose Beretta was ready on the mark. Mara could see Steve and Judy plainly between the ferns to her left, and Jane to her right. Steve would fire before she could get another line on Jane, but she went through the drill anyway, just in case.

Sometimes, a just in case comes in handy. Other times, it's as useless as any other exercise. This was another time. Judy pushed Steve's arm upward and brought out her stupid revolver. Mara shifted to a point-and-shoot at Judy just as Steve's Beretta boomed, sending ceiling dust onto the reception desk. Judy died, and Jane ran out of the hotel and into the Rivercenter shopping mall.

Mara followed her. It was not hard to do. Jane was tall and had covered her beautiful cloud of brown hair with an orange turban arrangement that stood out above the crowd like a beacon.

Jane ran out of an exit beneath the IMAX Theater with Mara no more than ten meters behind her. They ran into the Manger Hotel, past the reception desk, through the old corridor, and onto the staircase. Jane climbed to the fourth floor, looking back once. She found a service door, locked. Mara was at the end of the hall, lifting the Glock. Jane fired twice at Mara, wildly, to keep her down and then once more at the lock. The door opened to a steep staircase leading to the roof. She took it.

Jane's magazine held only eight rounds, and these were gone. Her spares were still on the bed in room 557 where Charlie had put them when he thought she would come with him. Damn that girl, she thought. Mara was a positive professional hazard. Jane waited for her on the roof and evened out the match with a well-timed kick that knocked the Glock out of Mara's hand and off the roof.

Mara rolled away, losing the wire in her ear, and when Jane landed beside her, used a sweep to take her down, but Jane was up again and away before she could make this minor victory a major one. Jane came at her, preparing a punching combination that Mara could see a mile away. Jane was slow, her training not as thorough, but she had limbs far longer than Mara's, more strength, and greater weight. Mara could not get in close enough to land anything effective.

Jane could not land anything, either, because Mara was too fast and seemed to read her mind. Every lunge landed on air.

Mara's entire body was involved in every move. Hatred impelled her, without dilution, without reason. There were plenty of causes; Jane was a proven enemy, a devious one, and formidable, but the hatred had nothing to do with any of that. It was a pure intensity of physical, chemical, and mental concentration. She hated the person who was trying to kill her. Mara intended to win or die. There were no reservations in her, no restrictions.

They moved naturally to the edge of the roof, and the idea occurred to them both simultaneously. Mara's plan, though, was one grain more devious. She teetered at the edge and watched Jane gather herself for a big push. The tall woman came toward her, giving her enough time to read a manual of martial arts. Mara waited for her and then helped her over the side.

Celebration would have to wait. She saw them from the corner of her eye and had only sufficient time to break the chain and drop her lucky charm before they were on her. A signal, she thought, but she doubted anybody would look for her up here.

She was forced face down onto the roof, her arms tied behind her, her mouth taped shut. She was blindfolded. They half pushed, half carried, her down a metal staircase at the side of the building. She tried not to think about the height, was grateful she couldn't see it. At the bottom, she felt herself seized and thrown onto a metal floor, heard a door slam behind her, and felt movement. She was in a vehicle of some kind. Her ankles were being tied. There were instructions given in Russian. She understood them.

"Begin procedures," said a voice.

THIRTY-FIVE

Charlie and Steve were the first to come back.

"Where is Frank?" asked Seal. He could smell the cordite and the blood, and he did not dare ask about Mara.

John had no such reservations. "Where is Mara?"

Steve answered Seal's question. "Frank is fucking running rings around that cop. He's a damned good babysitter. Call Misha and Louis. Now. Tell them to meet us somewhere. Now. Jay said he had a safehouse for us. That will do. John, get your black bag."

Charlie sat on a folding chair and began peeling off the layers of his suit: coat, tie, holster, shirt, armor, undershirt. John knelt beside him and probed the wound in his side, across and between the ribs.

Seal spoke to Louis on the radio and punched Jay's directions to the safehouse into the computer. When Frank came in, Seal gave him the address and put him in the driver's seat. He stood by the computer as they lurched out of the parking lot. The air conditioning blew a few empty coffee cups off the top of the screen but made no headway in the heat that had built up from baking for ten minutes in the South Texas sun.

Steve and Sergei sat across from each other at the table. Charlie sat at the end of the table facing them, the doctor dabbing at his side. Steve put an elbow on the table, held his forehead in the palm of one hand, and let a gold chain drop to the table from his other hand.

Seal lost it then. He blamed that pussy-whipped asshole Charlie, pure and simple, and he would make the sucker pay. He would fucking grind him into the coffee stains on the floor. Seal was lucky that Charlie was wheezing and partly disarmed. He was lucky, but not sorry. Charlie got in some good licks, but so did he. Steve and Sergei held them apart and they continued the battle in screams.

"What the fuck were you doing? Trying to turn the enemy just because she has tits! You son of a bitch!"

"Why did you let her go out? Why didn't you keep her here with you?"

"What the fuck was I supposed to do, Charlie? She's a specialist. I'm a babysitter. We both did our jobs. I supported her and she saved your sorry ass, yours and Steve's."

"You don't know that."

"I do know that. You're sittin' here, stuck like a pig but still breathin'. You shoulda never gone out on that goatfuck and you know it!"

Sergei joined the discussion. "You should have let me go after her!" he shouted at Seal.

"To do what? You think you could save her when Charlie and Steve couldn't? What are you, the fucking kung fu kid?"

John stood up between the parties. "I need some room here to work and some information. Steve, why don't you pour us all some scotch?"

The first round went down right away, the second more slowly. While he sipped his second cup, Charlie briefed them, gasping and puffing at intervals.

"We cleared the room with no problems," he said. "I took half a dozen weapons off Jane: a primary, a backup, three spare magazines, a couple of knives. I put them on the bed. Steve took the cartridges out of Judy's .357 and let her carry the gun empty because she wouldn't leave the room without it. He took her downstairs to the lobby. I told Jane we would give him five minutes to dump her and then meet him behind the hotel."

Charlie paused to drink and catch his breath.

"Jane kissed me. To pass the time, she said. I felt her hand come up my right side, where the armor does not meet. It was an odd movement, but her hand was nowhere near my gun on the left, so I was slow to be alerted. Then I heard somebody banging at the door. I turned suddenly and felt something cold rip the flesh over my rib. Whatever it was went in above the rib, but I was alerted by this time and able to stop Jane's hand. There was more pounding on the door. Jane wriggled free from me, grabbed her primary off the bed, and ran for the door. She opened it and fired two rounds towards the hall before running out. I drew my Glock, but I was tangled in a bedspread that had been on the floor. I took the knife out of my side. It was an eight-inch stiletto. Two inches were bloody."

"Only two?" asked John. "You're sure?"

Charlie nodded and gasped for air. "I saw someone look inside, then run after Jane. The light was behind her, so I did not know it was Mara. I followed but couldn't catch my breath enough to run. I heard a shot in the lobby and got there in time to see Steve running through the mall. I followed him but lost him in the crowd. I left the mall through an exit that faced another hotel. There was a street to my right. A crowd had gathered in it. I pushed through and found Jane at the center. She was dead. Her legs were broken. She must have fallen. Steve pushed through to me and began pulling me out of the crowd. A policeman stopped us. Frank came out of nowhere and played his US Government official line. He was brilliant."

"Thank you," came a voice from behind the curtain. Frank pulled the RV into the driveway of a house on a residential street. It was a fairly well-to-do neighborhood, with large trees and manicured lawns, but the houses were older, and graffiti decorated the wooden fences at the end of the block.

The safehouse had a heavy door with good locks. The perimeter was covered by motion and infrared sensors. The house also had three toilets and two showers, a full refrigerator, and a large dining room table. John claimed first use of the table. He put Charlie on it and widened the wound enough to get at the lung to repair a nick. In the first five minutes, there was no mention of Mara. Mack and Louis came in and sat on dining room chairs, watching without expression as John worked. Sergei held Charlie's shoulders down.

While John stitched the muscles in Charlie's side, Steve began his briefing. "Judy talked my fucking ear off in that lobby. I heard Mara shout my name and I knew it was a warning, so I rolled and came back to my feet as two rounds whizzed right past me. I had my gun in my hand and pointed in the direction the shots came from when Jane stepped out from behind a tree. I had her. Shit. I had her, and that bitch Judy bumped my arm up, so I shot the fucking ceiling. Then she pulls out an empty revolver. How stupid can you get? There wasn't a damn thing I could do for her. She was down before I could blink, and I saw Jane heading for the door and Mara going after her. I ran after Mara. I lost her but kept going to the other end of the mall. I found a door and went through it. Mara's Glock hit the sidewalk in front of me. It almost beaned me." He pulled it out of his pocket and handed it to Mack.

Mack looked at it, still without expression.

"I figured it came from the roof of an old hotel in front of me. The windows were all shut, and I couldn't see shit going on. I went inside and climbed the stairs. I found an access door on the fourth floor with the lock blown off. It led to the roof. The stairs were steep like a ladder. While I was climbing, I heard scraping sounds on the roof, but when I got there, there was nothing. No sound. Nobody. I heard people in the street below, ran to the edge, and saw Jane smashed in the street. There was something shiny on the roof. I picked this up." He handed Mack Mara's lucky charm.

Everybody had gathered near the table. Some sat on a long, low counter that separated the dining room from the kitchen. Others were in chairs. Sergei and Seal stood. Everybody watched Mack and Louis. They did not move. Mack gazed at the gold chain and charm in his hand, then looked up at Steve. "Go on," he said.

"I decided I would run to all four sides of the roof," said Steve. "At the very first one, to the left of where I found the charm, there was a fire escape to the street. I saw a green van below me. It pulled out and squealed around the corner."

John finished the dressing, and Charlie got off the table and repeated his account for Mack and Louis.

He received the same quiet attention. The doctor took a chair next to Seal in a corner. Nobody seemed to be breathing. The violence in the RV had been less creepy than this airless stillness.

When Charlie finished, Mack put Mara's Glock in his pocket and gave the chain to Louis. He pulled his chair to the center of the table and began pointing to people and then to places at the table where he wanted them to sit. Everybody did as they were told. With alacrity. Louis sat next to him, Sergei across from him. Charlie and Steve sat on either side of Sergei. Mack put Frank at one end of the table, and Jay at the other. He did not point to Seal or the doctor, and they did not volunteer to move from their corner. Anyway, the only places left at the table were next to Mack and Louis. Nobody wanted to get that close.

Mack took off his coat, loosened his tie, and looked at his watch. "It requires twenty-five minutes to reach the warehouse from downtown. They should be there just now. I assume they are going there?" He looked at Sergei, who swallowed and nodded.

He looked at Jay. "What about FBI presence? Will they be there?"

"I'm afraid not," said Jay. "I took a look at some of the message traffic in the local office. The Special Agent-In-Charge here is a friend of mine, though he doesn't work for me. The word he got from Justice was to support this guy's operation with watchers and intelligence, but to stay out of his way."

"Then Maximovich is free to do as he pleases." Mack looked at Sergei again. "Begin with the extraction itself. You are Maximovich. Begin with procedures."

THIRTY-SIX

S ergei spoke quickly. "If there was only one van, then he is using one team. This was an opportunity, not planned, so there must have been only one team available. Place the subject on the ground, in this case on the roof. One ties the hands, another tapes the mouth, a third the blindfold. They must get her off the roof, so they will leave the legs free until she is down. In the van, the legs are tied, with a connecting rope to the wrists to restrict movement."

He paused. Then he continued as if reading from a textbook. "Check her for weapons. Check her everywhere. Remove the tape to check the mouth if it has not been done. Replace with fresh tape."

"Will Maximovich do this himself?" asked Mack.

"No. A subordinate will do it and tell him that… she is innocent."

"And when they come to the warehouse?" Mack looked at his watch again. "They are there now."

Sergei looked him in the eye.

"He will rape her immediately."

"And the others?"

Sergei hesitated. "No. Not until the interrogation."

Mack looked at Seal. "What was she wearing?"

"The blue knit outfit, white sandals, body armor."

Back to Sergei. "Will he strip her?"

"Only what's necessary. Apart from cutting the leg ropes, no. Not until interrogation."

"When will that be? Why not interrogate now?"

Sergei hesitated again and looked away. "He will be eager to set a trap for you. He knows he will need every moment to prepare."

"How does he know we know where they are?"

Sergei looked at his hands on the table. "I gave her a ring. It once belonged to my great-grandmother. Volodya knows the ring. When he sees it, he will know that I am with you and that I will give you the location. He will want to be ready."

Louis spoke. "She was taught not to wear jewelry at such times. This charm from Vasily was an exception." He looked at Seal. "Did she take the ring off?"

"I didn't know she had a ring."

John spoke up. "No," he said. "She wore it. I saw it." He kept his face expressionless in the unwelcome heat of Mack's stare.

"If it delays the interrogation," said Mack, "it is good news." He held out his hand to Jay, who put a large white roll of paper into it. He spread the paper on the table. It was a diagram of the warehouse. "Now, Sergei, set the trap for us. Procedures."

Sergei stood over the table and considered this. "I will put her in the center rear of the warehouse, on the floor, not in the offices." He pointed at the large white space on the paper. "I assume you will come in through the large doors at the front. I may even leave them open for you. I want to make you run the gauntlet. I will take the tape off her mouth, I want her to tell you where she is, and I will leave her body armor in place so that my snipers don't kill her too soon. Then, I will have her hug a crate. Semianov told me that the back portion of the warehouse contains mostly crates. Old Dunovski taught us to make rescues as complicated as possible. Tie everything separately, he said. If you tie her hands and feet to opposite sides of a packing crate, the cutter must negotiate at least three faces of the crate, at each face will be a sniper, behind good cover. With two ropes to cut on each side, a rescuer will not survive." Sergei looked up from the paper. "There are only four of you."

"How many of them?"

"Volodya traveled with five teams, so that is thirty, plus drivers and extra watchers, but these are useless as fighters. You destroyed one team in the desert, and Charlie and Mara decimated another, leaving three teams intact and two extras."

"And where would you place these twenty men?"

"Besides at the sniper positions, I would put them throughout the building but especially on the cat-walks. Once you enter, they can watch your progress and support the others on the floor, who will try to converge on you when they hear firing and can determine your position. I doubt that more than one or two of you will make it to the snipers."

There was a long silence.

Charlie finally broke it. He held his forehead in one hand, the elbow on the table. "I made a terrible mistake. I am sorry."

"So it is your first," said Louis. "Your father made a dozen mistakes by your age."

"That is an exaggeration," said Mack.

"None was this disastrous," insisted Charlie.

"One was nearly so," said Mack. "It cost Vasily a portion of his liver."

Charlie looked up at his father. There was another long silence.

The doctor broke this one.

"Look, ah, I can use a knife. I can cut a rope. You could cover me or something like that."

"I can do that," said Seal, "and I can fire an MP5."

"So can I, for that matter," said Frank.

"Ditto." Jay raised his hand.

"They would cut you down within the first ten meters," said Louis.

"Not if someone ran silent point ahead of them," said Sergei. "While you keep them busy at one end of the building, we can run in at the other, find her, and cut the ropes. With four of them cutting, it will be fast enough. I will run silent point."

"These were your men," Mack told him. "How many have you ever killed?"

"There were the two I shot the other day."

"And you think you can run silent? One hesitation and you will all die."

"I killed plenty of the VC in Nam," said Seal.

"That was twenty-five years ago and in battle. There is a difference."

"Uh. this is going to be a fucking battle," said Seal defiantly.

Mack rubbed his forehead. He looked at John, sat back in his chair, and loosened his tie again. The leather of his holster creaked as he shifted. "Doctor," he began, "I must say something to you especially, but this applies to all of you." He looked at Jay, Seal, and Frank in turn. "Your intentions are noble. I acknowledge that you are brave, but in your case, Doctor, also a little stupid. I tell you again, this is not television. Mara is not the pure maiden held by a dragon. She is a specialist who knew precisely what the risks were when she began this operation and when she went up on that roof. She does not expect anyone but her team to risk anything for her.

"You have known her for a few hours. If you succeed in helping to rescue her, and that is not likely, and if you live, which is even less likely, you will probably not see her again. You are a fine surgeon and a good man, Doctor, but I do not think you will win her. I am being very truthful. I will use whoever offers to help, but some of us will die. Each of you must make this decision in the understanding that it will probably be you and that it may be for nothing."

"We're all in, Mack," said Frank. "Let's not waste time. What's your plan?"

Mack took a pen out of his shirt pocket and used it to point at the diagram on the table. "They expect the team to go in together, through a door. We will climb to the roof, use plastique to blow holes in the roof—Sergei said he can prepare them—and fast rope down in four places onto the catwalks, firing as we descend." He pointed to points at roughly the four corners of the main part of the building.

"They are expecting to see four of us, so we must not disappoint them." He pointed the pen at Sergei. "You will be the fourth. If you hesitate on the catwalk, you kill only yourself. I hope. You go in here, near the safe, and make your way to the file. Louis will be on the other side of the front of the building. He will move to support you. Steve, here at the back, and Charlie at the other side."

"And you, Misha?" asked Louis.

"I will lead the babysitters in through this door, here." He pointed to a small door marked at the back of the building, labeled offices. "I will run silent point.

Once we find Mara and cut her free, I will lead them out by the closest door."

Louis studied the paper and looked at Charlie. "Can you climb twenty meters with fifteen kilos of full body armor and weapons? You still do not breathe well."

"I can do it."

"Can you fast rope down ten meters, firing?"

"Of course." The wheezing was audible.

Mack looked at the Doctor. "Can he?"

"He's in very good shape. It's amazing what a man can do when he has to."

"Can he, Doctor? I need your professional opinion."

"I don't see how he can."

Charlie threw him an eyeful of venom.

Mack rubbed his chin and shook his head, thinking.

"Papa. I can run point." Charlie's voice was quiet.

Mack stared.

"I have done it before, when we got out of Tbilisi."

Sergei nodded. "It's true."

There was an awkward silence.

Mack looked tired. He rested his arms on the table in front of him, as if worn out, and sighed. "Then you will be point."

Steve cleared his throat. "Ahem. If the babysitters are coming in here," he pointed at the back door on the paper, "and coming through my area under the catwalk over here, then I'm going to shoot them, because I'm going to shoot anything that fucking moves, except for Seal, maybe, in his dippy shirt. I can see that stupid shirt a mile away."

"Do you have more of these shirts, Seal?" asked Mack.

He nodded.

"All babysitters and the doctor will wear one of Seal's shirts."

"Give me about seven meters in front of the first shirt, Steve," said Charlie. "Do not shoot at movement in that space."

"Sensors?" Mack asked Louis.

"I will take care of them."

"May I make a request?" said Jay. "Once Mara is free, I would like to move to the safe. It will help if I ever have to testify in court that I can say I saw the list in such and such a place and removed it from same. It would be best if I am there when the safe is opened. Of course, I know it will depend on how it goes with Mara."

"If Mara is able," Mack told Charlie, "tell her to lead the others out. You take Jay to the safe."

Charlie nodded.

The neighborhood was nearly deserted in the early afternoon heat as they walked out to the RV. Only two boys on bicycles watched them leave. Jay Turner pulled John back to the end of the procession.

"You can stay in this house safely and I can get you out on the next flight, Doctor."

John looked at him in horror.

"You can stay on the RV and support the operation from there if you must help," Jay insisted.

Horror was fast becoming anger.

"I don't mean to insult you, Doctor. I'm just trying to keep you alive."

THIRTY-SEVEN

John did not regret his decision, but he complained like everybody else. Seal's shirts smelled like fetid mustard. They should turn up the air. Complaining was important. It made him feel alive, a precious feeling he savored.

"I am not wearing full body armor," Louis said in French.

Steve put it back in the shower and pulled out his full armor.

"Louis, we have discussed this," said Mack.

"I must climb a pole to set the fuse and cut the power, sprint two hundred meters, roll under the sensors, disable the backup generator, and sprint fifty meters to my rope. Then, I am only beginning, and you want me to wear an extra fifteen kilos. No, thank you. We never wore that crap in the old days, and we survived."

"We were constantly shot to pieces. And we could never attempt this."

"I don't like all this modern nonsense. I am more effective without it. I will wear the soft armor to make you feel better."

Charlie also wore the lighter soft body armor under his black shirt. John noticed nobody said anything about that.

Somebody handed him Steve's soft armor. Jay had his own and Frank wore Mack's, considerably adjusted. Seal hoped for luck; there was nothing to fit him. Mack, Sergei, and Steve looked like a human armada, with full body armor over their black clothing, vests over the armor, Kevlar balaclavas, and in the vests, spare magazines, ropes, and small, neat packages of plastic explosive, detonators arranged by Sergei. They also carried an assortment of handguns and knives along with Heckler & Koch MP5 submachine guns, two each, strapped across their backs.

Everybody received a wire and the radios were tested. Charlie handed John a Spyderco knife and a wire cutter, in case they had her tied with cables. Jay and the two babysitters each had an MP5 and a spare magazine in every pants pocket. There was a short debate about giving the doctor a gun. Seal objected; the doctor was directly behind him in the lineup. The idea didn't go anywhere.

"Once we're in, we use hand signals only," Charlie briefed them. "Silence must be perfect."

"Won't there be all kinds of shooting?" asked John. "Who cares if we make a noise in that?"

The other four stared at him until Frank answered. "They won't be expecting a bunch of babysitters coming in just to cut the ropes, Doctor. We don't want to announce ourselves. We want them to concentrate on the team coming down from the roof."

"And it's a fucking rule of nature that the smallest sound will find a nanosecond of silence," said Seal.

"Oh." John sensed that he was supposed to know what they planned to do about the snipers, so he did not ask any more questions.

...

John craned his neck around Seal's fat head, trying to see beyond it to the Kevlar balaclava that covered Charlie's. Behind him, he heard Frank breathing and Jay shifting his weight as they leaned against the wall in the shadows. Behind them, the RV was parked for what Steve called a quick egress.

Steve was now halfway up the face of the back wall of the warehouse, fifty meters ahead of them. The other three specialists—even Charlie now referred to Sergei as a specialist—were also on ropes at the same level as Steve. This was the office end of the building. It had windows in it but was judged the safest approach for them because no other building looked onto it.

Charlie's team waited in the shadows until Steve gave the signal from the rooftop. Then they moved forward. The door was locked. Charlie brought out a narrow tool and opened it quietly. The first room was empty and dim, with only a thin stream of daylight from a high window. They walked to the opposite end. Charlie stopped and gave them all a murderous look, telling them with signs to pick up their feet. The shuffles had been deafening, even through the noise of explosions on the roof and the beginning of a gun battle.

They made it to the warehouse floor. They made it around the first crate, ten feet past the last office. John could see the catwalk on the far wall to his right and a constant flash from something moving around on it. He did not have time to look up to his left, but the sounds of gunfire were constant there and in the distance toward the front of the building.

Charlie gave them the signal to crawl. John tried to crawl quietly, though the gun battle filled his skull with both primary and echoed booming, making him unsure what was noisy and what was not. In the next five feet, he learned what running silent point meant. His hand stuck in a warm puddle, and he saw a bloodless corpse not more than three feet away, the carotid still glistening. John understood, finally, what Charlie planned to do about the snipers. He followed the ballooning form of Seal in front of him. They paused, two, then three, times, and after each pause, they passed another body, though these had been killed more bloodlessly, which is a relative term, he thought, in the circumstances.

Windows high above the catwalk and the holes in the roof allowed them enough daylight to see where they were going, but their crate canyon route kept them in perpetual gloom, welcome when they were moving, terrifying when they sat waiting.

They waited again in the murk. John heard Mack's voice shouting.

Mara's voice rang out. "Don't! It's a trap!" It was not far away.

"Of course it's a trap, you silly girl," muttered Seal.

"Silence!" Charlie's whisper came over the wire. They could not see him. "Left, then forward," came the next whispered order.

They stopped again. To his left, John could see a shape sitting high on a box, supporting what looked like a broom handle over the lip of another box. A dark form moved toward it from behind. The forms converged, the second laid the first one down and caught the broom—John recognized a rifle—before it hit the floor. Charlie slid off the box and gave them the hand signal to wait. Seal acknowledged. Charlie disappeared to the right.

They squatted along a long wall of crates and boxes leading to the dead sniper. This time was the longest wait. Altogether, they had been inside the warehouse for two minutes, by John's watch, yet this wait seemed to have gone on for hours already. They heard a steady foot-pound and pushed themselves closer to the boxes behind them, wishing they were chameleons. The steps became louder and were coming from an aisle that opened to the left and in front of Seal.

The man rounding the corner got over his surprise quickly. He swung his submachine gun in a wide arc, firing as it moved. John watched as the bullets hit the concrete floor, ping, ping, ping, chewing up little bits of concrete and puffs of concrete dust, as each pit appeared a foot closer to Jay on John's right.

Everything was clear and slow, yet John had no time to think about it before the noise exploded next to him and he was hit by something hot. He looked at his arm. There was no blood. Pieces of brass were scattered at his feet and Seal's gun was spewing more. The man in the aisle was dead.

"Shit!" said Charlie.

"Had to," said Seal. "I got him."

"You're going to have twenty more. Keep them busy."

Frank took his Walther PPK from under his shirt and put it in John's right hand. He molded the fingers of his left hand around the bottom of the right and made him sit on the floor, knees up, forearms between the knees. He moved the wire away from his mouth. "Point that way," he whispered in his ear, moving

John's hands until the Walther was pointing at the intersecting aisle. "If you see anything, squeeze the trigger."

John glanced at Seal on his left, who nodded. They heard the sound of several feet running. In the next instant, the gun battle was a reality, a practical occupation, not an abstraction. He smelled the cordite, heard the constant boom in every aural nerve, saw the muzzle flashes, his friends' and his enemies', and felt the Walther throw him into the crate behind him every time an enemy poked his nose out of that aisle. He hit nothing but crates, and occasionally the floor, but the enemy behind that corner could not stay long enough to take aim.

"Now!" came Charlie's voice over the wire.

John wanted to ask, "Now what?" But Frank was already nudging him to follow Seal to the left.

Frank followed, facing backward. Jay moved in front and to the right of John, firing into the aisle until they cleared it. They sprinted then, firing behind them occasionally, following the constant stream of Seal's gun. He stopped firing as they flew around a corner and there in front of them sat a single, narrow crate. They were at its empty face. On the left-hand face, John saw fingers.

He took a step toward the fingers. Seal yanked him back and pushed him to the right side of the crate. John saw a rifle barrel extending over his head from the top of a taller crate. A dark head moved behind it. John raised the Walther. Seal slapped his hand.

"No, stupid. That's Charlie."

Charlie fired and they cut. There was a lot of rope, much of it tied in independent knots. John had an ankle. Seal cut the rope around the wrist above him. There was a burst of submachine gun fire from behind them. John heard the boom of Charlie's answer. Another burst came from their left. John was almost through. The knife slipped in his hand, and he realized his hand was wet. He gripped it tighter and cut the last strand. Her foot moved back immediately. Seal's knife fell on the floor by his knees and the wetness was everywhere. Seal leaned on him, and John struggled to shrug him off. He knelt high on his knees and finished cutting the last few strands around her wrist.

She was beside him in the next instant, cradling Seal's lifeless head in her hands. She kissed his forehead and picked up the MP5 at his side.

Charlie, Frank, and Jay were already there. Charlie handed her three spare magazines. She put them in the belt under her blouse and slipped the wire he gave her into her ear.

"Jay and I are going to the safe. You take them out."

She nodded.

They met Mack on the way. He took over from her as point.

They stumbled onto the backs of at least seven men firing into a cubicle formed by eight-foot safes. Mara and Mack shot most of them in the back. Only one or two had time to turn around. Inside the cubicle, they found Louis, smiling. He sat in a snug corner under an iron shelf. John could feel the heat from his gun. Mack moved his wire and spoke into Mara's ear. She nodded and left the cubicle, pulling John behind her. They ran for a green exit sign.

Outside was just that. It was outside. Glorious, sunny, blinding, hot, free, safe. John ran beside Mara. He could still hear gunfire coming from the building beside them. They ran to the RV. Once inside, he wanted to kiss her, to celebrate. He wanted to shout and whoop and beat his chest. He was not only alive; he wasn't even hurt. She climbed into the cab before he could catch her, started the engine, and set them on a course careening toward the front of the building. He fell against the table as they turned. She shouted at him to put the table away.

"Make it into a bed," she said.

"A what? Oh." He folded up the table and pulled out the seats, making one seamless single bed.

They skidded to a stop. She set the brake but left the engine running.

"Get your bag," she said as she threw open the door.

He brought both eyebrows together in a 'v' over his nose.

"Louis is hit," she explained. "Louis is hit bad."

And the euphoria was gone. He could barely move his arm to pick up the bag. Seal was gone. John looked down at the shirt he wore. He only met these guys a few days ago and they felt like an anvil in his stomach. Mack came through the door, supporting Louis behind him. Frank pushed from behind. They put the Frenchman diagonally on the bed because it was too short for him.

John tried to pull Louis's black shirt away from the wounds in his side. He could see the entry holes in the wet fabric, black and red. Louis grabbed his wrist with incredible strength, said "No," soundlessly, and looked at him with an expression that reminded John of a patient he once had as an intern.

She had been a middle-aged woman, terminal with cancer, who would not let the nurse insert a catheter for a test he'd ordered. "You're not touching me," she said to him when he tried. He called in two orderlies to restrain her while the nurse did her job. The memory made John close his eyes in shame.

He opened them again when Mara touched his sleeve. She held the box of morphine vials. He drew up the dose. Louis let him administer that.

Charlie and Jay both fell through the door, Charlie wheezing, Jay bleeding. Jay held to his chest a flat packet, the size of a patient's chart, in a zippered black plastic pouch.

Mack took the pouch from Jay and waited while Charlie lay on the floor, finding breath. "Where is Steve?"

Charlie shook his head. He didn't know.

"Sergei?"

"Reminiscing with Maximovich." Jay pushed his back up against the seat. He pressed his right thigh and blood seeped through his fingers. John brought his bag over. It was a jagged wound, deep and bloody, but major vessels and bones were not involved. John pulled out a splinter of wood, cleaned the wound, and began stitching.

Jay made him stop and crawled to the open door. John followed him, protesting. Frank said, "Shhh!"

Charlie picked up his rifle and used it to help himself up. He pulled the curtains off the window next to the RV door, opened the louvered glass, and used the barrel to break through the screen on the outside. The entire screen came off in one piece and clattered to the ground.

The attraction was a silent, rolling battle that poured out from the loading door at the front of the warehouse, off the loading ramp, and onto the broken cement in front of them. Sergei and his friend Volodya were locked together in a mutual determination to annihilate each other. Maximovich's face and neck glowed red, glistening with sweat. Veins and muscles bulged in Sergei's neck as he held Maximovich's wrist and tried to twist the gun out of his hand. They each scrambled for a foothold, first Maximovich on the bottom, then Sergei. Sergei's left hand remained locked on that wrist, but his right sought an opening, any opening, in which to do damage.

Mack looked at Charlie, who shook his head. No clear shot.

Sergei found his opening. Maximovich's gun fell out of his hand as he flew backward into the raised loading dock. Sergei landed a kick to the chest and Maximovich's back hit the concrete with a thwack. He fell, sitting up. Sergei held a knife to his throat. They could see only half of Maximovich's face and in that half, defeat.

Sergei paused, then turned and put the knife away, laughing, and began walking the seven remaining meters to the RV.

Maximovich began to move.

"No!" whispered Mara.

"I can't get him. Sergei's in the way," said Charlie.

Volodya stretched himself to the right, grabbed the gun, staggered to a stand, and pointed it at Sergei's back.

They heard a single shot.

Sergei turned; Volodya fell. Steve stood swaying in the doorway on one leg and lowered his Beretta.

"Pavlenko, you son of a bitch, there was no fucking catwalk in my corner. Get your stupid ass over here and help me."

...

The RV rolled away from the warehouse twelve minutes after Charlie first picked the lock.

THIRTY-EIGHT

Twelve-year-old single malt scotch made the rounds and Mara was grateful for it. She sat on the floor by Louis's bed, holding his hand as he slept. She did not sip the amber liquid in the white Styrofoam cup, she drank it in hungry gulps. One, two, and it was gone.

The RV took a sharp turn in the road, rolling Louis on his side. He groaned in his sleep. He was not gone, but he was going. Mara watched the doctor's face as he inspected the neat, round holes in Louis's side, where the soft body armor did not meet. John's lips were pressed together. They became seamless as he took the pulse. He gazed at the skin. It had a yellow tinge. He looked under an eyelid, then turned away quickly without looking her in the eye. She began to cry, silently, allowing only a few tears at a time.

Misha was on the computer arranging their egress. He called their pilots on the satellite link up and told them to bring the jet to an airfield in Mexico.

John sewed up Jay's leg as the FBI man made frantic phone calls on the cellular, cashing in chips, he told one person. He was beginning to sound like Frank.

John sounded like Steve. He called Mara away from Louis to assist because these scissors were fucking useless, that needle was a piece of shit. Jay covered the phone with one large hand and pleaded with her with his eyes: come and help this doctor before these people hang up on me. She helped and John was quiet, but still ruthlessly exacting. She gave up the idea of having him look at her back whenever the dust might settle. Jay gasped more than once, despite the local anesthetic, but of course, the stitches in his leg were flawless.

Setting Steve's broken leg was a wrestling match and a profanity contest. Mara had no idea that so many of Seal's words could be strung together so artfully, the same word used as noun, verb, adjective, and adverb in the same sentence. John held his own in the word battle and managed to hit Steve twice physically, in the stomach and chest, for fucking interfering with fucking medical treatment, he screamed, as Sergei held Steve's arms and shoulders to prevent the reply. Mara wondered if the word was used here first as a helping or linking verb, or was it a gerund? She decided it was a participle modifying the gerund 'interfering'. And the second was certainly an adjective.

Misha had a ricochet round in his arm. He told John to go away.

John approached Michael cautiously. Mara's brother sat on the floor with his back against the refrigerator and his feet stretched out before him. His lips were blue, and he breathed in short, noisy gasps. He held his rifle across his lap. Dried blood caked his fingernails.

It is as difficult to see a loved one through a stranger's eyes as it is to look in the mirror and pretend you see someone else. A magic mirror might tell a few truths, but these are hard to come by. Michael was revealed to Mara through the change in John's eyes. Two days before, the doctor had been careless, confident, and even impudent with everyone he met. Now, he showed more respect around Misha, a thing remarkable only because it took him so long to catch on. But with Michael, he was more than respectful; he was careful.

The stitches in Michael's chest had torn out and three ribs were broken. The soft body armor had taken six rounds. The lung repair held, though, and Michael found it easier to breathe once the ribs were bound.

Mara sat next to her brother and handed bandages to the doctor until every movement of every finger required every last effort from her. She slumped against Michael's undamaged side and laid her head against his shoulder, staring at John without

seeing him, seeing only the ridiculous shirt that tent-
ed him in green, yellow, apricot, and azure, like a
painter's smock, a painter more than normally clumsy.
The shirt reminded her that Seal was gone, and the
tears began again, more noisily than before because
she did not have the strength to control anything. Nor
did she have energy for a full deluge, so when
Michael put his arm around her shoulder, she took
the comfort offered and promptly fell asleep with
him, blocking the aisle with two bodies no one dared
disturb.

She did not sleep long. Her back was on fire, a fire
hotter than the one that had burned it, and every
bump in the road moved the floor, refrigerator, her
brother, her body armor, the bandages, in a chain reaction that scraped each wound, deep or shallow,
adding friction to the flames.

Michael was sick beside her, and it triggered the
same response in her. She dabbed at the mess on her
skirt until it occurred to her to just take the thing off.
She had put on a pair of jeans under the skirt as soon
as she climbed into the RV because Maximovich had
cut away her underwear. The skirt was redundant.

She thought she was doing all of this gracefully,
but it woke Michael and attracted John and Sergei.
She said no, but they made her let the doctor look at
her back. He dabbed something cool on it and stuck
in a needle and everything felt better. She fell asleep
again.

The RV was slowing down when Mara woke the second time. She stood up and leaned on the computer. Jay had opened the black curtain behind the cab and was standing behind it, steadying himself at the comm bank. Mara read the sign as they entered a place called Hondo. "This is God's Country," said the sign. "Please don't drive through it like hell." They drove through this piece of Texas heaven, past a golf course, and onto an airfield. Jay directed Frank to a metal hangar where two men were sliding the doors open. Frank drove inside, and the doors squealed as they closed after them.

Nothing now was good, right, or pleasant. Everybody bumped, groaned, and swore, at life, at each other, at themselves. There was an argument Mara did not even try to understand. She was disgusted. There was nothing to look forward to. The flight home, the cool mountains, a hot bath, were all too far away to appeal or to lessen the prospect of the burning in her back at every next moment. Yet that was not the worst of it. Her heart had been dipped in hot lead and as it cooled it dropped, gaining mass and weight until she thought she could never carry it all. Seal was forever gone. Louis was going. And Sergei?

Sergei was talking to Misha.

Misha said something to John and John led her by the arm out of the RV. She needed a walk, he told her.

They strolled around the hangar looking at antique airplanes without seeing them. She saw Sergei and Misha step out of the RV and around to the other side, out of her sight.

John stopped by an airplane engine on a maintenance stand. Oil dripped into a bucket on the floor. Mara stuck her finger in the oil drip absently.

"I ..." said John.

She looked at him and waited. Her tears had streaked the dirt into striped rivulets down her face. There was blood and now oil on her powder blue knit blouse.

John wanted her more than ever, but she did not see his longing through the multicolored hues of his face. She did not see much of anything through the litany of names that sang the grief in her soul, Seal, Louis, Sergei.

She was unprepared when he took a deep breath and said, "Will you marry me?"

"Oh, John, you flatter me too much." *Was he blind?*

"That means no."

Was there a hint of relief there?

"But what would you do with me?" she said. "Think, John. Where would you put me? Imagine me as a doctor's wife. It should make you shudder. What will happen to your career if Mrs. Fleabottom insults the color of my shoes at a coffee morning? Think of the scandal. Surgeon's wife purees boss's wife. I won't have my shoes insulted, you know."

She grinned. She meant to cheer him, and such a smile would have improved any moment but this one. But she had added to his share of lead weight and could not help him carry it.

He looked away. She wiped an oily finger on her jeans.

"There is one other thing. Mack asked me to ask you," he said awkwardly, "to offer you medical help if... if there is damage...." He did not look at her.

"I'm sorry, John. I am sure Misha did not mean to put you in such a position. Please don't turn so red." She put her hand on his shoulder, smearing grease on Seal's shirt, and looked him directly in the eyes. "I am all right. You can tell Misha. Maximovich was about to, but he saw Sergei's ring." She held up the ring on her right hand. "He knew he did not have much time and he was smart enough to use every moment. He was very, very good, and would have succeeded if it weren't for you and the others, John. I owe you a great debt."

"What will you do?" he croaked. "Will you join the team?"

"I am on the team. But I will try to stay home at times like a good girl. Maybe I can make myself useful in the computer room."

She turned to the engine again, played with new oil on her fingertips. "Some victories are too expensive. Some victories are shams, deceits, chimeras that dissolve when you try to celebrate them." She looked at John, not noticing the tears that threatened his eyes because he was so good at stopping them.

"Misha is hard and sour and dutiful and danger-ous," she said. "But he is also right. My mother says that is the most infuriating thing about him. I agree. He says—he lectures me—that life is not always arranged the way we want it, that selflessness takes many forms, that boring old caution, like wearing your gun when you'd rather pretend you don't need it, or wearing full body armor even though it's heavy, or staying home when that's not very exciting, some-times takes the highest courage, is the greatest sacri-fice we can make for people who love us. I wish my father had made it. I wish Louis had made it. I will go home and try to behave myself."

John looked around the hangar, fighting the stu-pid tears. She saw them now, at the corners of his eyes. Jay and Frank counted money from a suitcase onto a small table, and the man selling his airplane counted it again.

The shot was not very loud, but it echoed in the metal building. Mara did not have John's control. Her tears fell immediately. The lead in her heart gathered mass, at least nine millimeters more, and her heart sank under the weight. She ran to the RV. John fol-lowed her, trying to reach her arm, tugging at her shirt, babbling something about waiting. They round-ed the far corner of the vehicle together.

Misha held his SIG at his side, and there was a new hole in a trash can near him. Sergei stood next to him. Mara threw her arms around Sergei and laughed and cried.

"He requested that I shoot him," said Misha. He shrugged and reholstered the SIG. "I missed."

Mara flung herself around Misha's neck, laughing with more tears and kissing his cheek. He smiled an almost smile and returned her hug.

"The bad guy is not supposed to get the girl," John said to Misha.

"I told you before, Doctor, this is not television."

EPILOGUE

Janine Fairfax tapped her finger impatiently on her breakfast plate.

"When do you suppose he will come downstairs?" she asked the newspaper across the table.

"Hmmm?" Her husband Jack put down one side of his paper. "Who is that, dear?"

"John. Our son. He has been asleep for three days now. And that eye! Are you sure he is all right? Could he have a brain concussion?" She pushed a wiry red curl away from her eyes. Another took its place.

"He is all right." John Fairfax, Senior, returned to his newspaper.

"But he does not talk about where he has been." She stared at the paper. There was no response. She

picked up the mail beside the butter and began leaf-
ing through it. She found a letter with no return addressed to her husband. It was postmarked Chicago.
She opened it.

Dear John,

*We landed safely in Mexico. Louis requested a priest
and was given the sacrament before we took off. He passed
away peacefully in our jet on the way home. Before he died,
he asked me to tell you he was sorry he hit you. He was
anxious for your forgiveness. He also wanted me to thank
you. You are the first man of peace he ever met, he said, who
truly behaved as a man.*

*We are healing quickly and send our deepest gratitude
and best wishes.*

With great fondness,

Mara

*P.S. Please remember how deadly a piece of paper can
be.*

Janine's brow was still furrowed over this puzzle
when her son plopped into the seat beside her. "Who
is Mara?" she asked.

He took the letter from her hand and read it
quickly. She watched his face change colors beneath
the yellow tint that surrounded one eye. He stood and
walked to the kitchen stove, lit one gas burner, and set
the letter on fire.

"What are you doing?" she asked.

Her husband put down the newspaper to watch
as their son dropped the charred corner of the page

into a pot of cold oatmeal. He left it there. He inspected the coffee pot, poured some old coffee into a dirty cup out of the sink, and sat down at the table. He wore the most horrible shirt Janine had ever seen. It was not only horrible, it was filthy, smelled to high heaven, and she was sure that some of the red-brown stains on it were blood. This did not particularly distress her as the wife and mother of surgeons, but she wished he would wash and shave. He stank.

"I'm glad to see you have emerged," she said. "Is Mara a girlfriend? Someone important?"

He did not answer.

She had another way to get a response.

"Clarissa Sonsten is coming over this afternoon. Mary Beth is in town, and I invited them both. You remember Clarissa's daughter, don't you? The pretty girl you took to the senior prom. She is a very successful lawyer now." She stopped when she saw him close his eyes and wince.

"Why do you keep trying to pair me up with women who are nothing like you, Mama? They all come off an assembly line. Suitable for doctor's wives. Conventional, rational, and above all, polite."

"She's a pretty girl, John."

"Yes. But what would she do if Mrs. Fleabottom insulted her shoes?"

"Who is Mrs. Fleabottom?"

His father put the paper down again to look at him. "We want grandchildren, John."

"Yes, Dad."

"Will you please make yourself presentable for the Sonstens, *mon cher*?

"Yes, Mama."

His father raised an eyebrow and squinted at the same time, a difficult maneuver for other faces, but not for one trained to freeze scrub nurses with a single glance over a mask.

"What makes you suddenly so agreeable, son?"

John shrugged. "I guess if I need somebody to plead for me, it may as well be a lawyer." He drained his cup and stood. On his way through the dining room, he suddenly leapt into the air, swinging his foot in a high arc and upsetting the lamp on the buffet.

"What are you doing?" Janine cried.

"Just wondering," he said, "if Mary Beth Sonsten can do a tornado kick."

The End

Will Mara be a good girl and stay out of danger at home? Or will she become a fully operational member of the team? Find out in the next Charlemagne File, *Vory*. Bookstore links are available here: https://books2read.com/u/m0orvJ.

Join the Charlemagne Files newsletter for more stories and information about the series, its world of covert operations, and the lives of the characters on the team. Join here: https://www.charlemagnefiles.com/contact.

If you enjoyed this book, please leave a short review at your favorite bookstore.

CHARLEMAGNE AND THE SEC-

TION

The fictional world of The Section follows a few conventions. It may help the first-time reader of The Charlemagne Files to know some of these.

Who/what/ where is The Section?

The Section is a department of an intelligence agency of the United States. Its employees are civil servants. It includes support staff members who provide identity documents, financial controls, and physical and document security. The offices are near the East Coast, maybe Virginia.

The operational agents are called babysitters. They arrange on-site logistical support for freelance specialists during operations. Most operations are not conducted within the United States, with some exceptions.

Babysitters themselves do not carry identity documents in their names during an operation and never carry any official identification from their organization. Their purpose is to allow the organization to deny any association with them or their mission.

Nicknames

Babysitters in The Section receive nicknames from their coworkers when they join the office. These names are often undesirable and used mercilessly among the members of the office. It is part of the team-building process in a stressful occupation.

Coins

Challenge coins are traditionally stamped with symbols or mottos that designate the intelligence unit of their owners. The tradition is that when members of the unit are present at the bar and one produces his coin, all must produce theirs. Anyone failing to show their coin is responsible for the bar tab. If all produce their coins, then the challenger who first produced his or her coin is responsible for the tab.

File designations

The highest classification of information is Top Secret. Beyond Top Secret, more sensitive information is strictly controlled in a number of ways including designation as Sensitive Compartmented Information

(SCI). This requires an additional clearance and often a named clearance based on Need-To-Know.

In The Section, files on specialists or specialist teams receive a one-word code name, printed across the file and restricted to very few people. When a solo or specialist team is employed on an operation, another designator word will refer to the operation and will be used for funding, reports, etc.

The Section's file name for Charlemagne is WEDGE. Thus CETUS WEDGE (second book of the Charlemagne Files) means an operation dubbed CETUS using the team called WEDGE.

Specialist

A team or solo operative used by Western governments for black operations conducted without fingerprints in high-risk situations expected to involve death.

GLOSSARY OF GAME NAMES

Charlemagne

Original Team

Mack: so dubbed by Western babysitters because he uses a knife at times; Austrian leader and decision maker of Charlemagne; called Misha by other members of his team; probable real name is Michael; last name is unknown.

The Frenchman: deceased marksman and technical expert of Charlemagne; real name is Louis; last name is unknown.

Vasily Sobieski: deceased explosives expert and martial artist whose father was a noted solo specialist; no aliases.

Later Team

Charlie Taylor: marksman; son of Mack; probable real name is Michael; last name unknown.

Steve Donovan: martial artist; former fighter pilot; abandoned real name was Daniel Martin Kessler.

Mara Sobieski Pavlenko: technical expert and marksman; daughter of Vasily Sobieski and biological daughter of Mack; wife of Sergei Pavlenko.

Sergei Pavlenko: explosives expert; former KGB babysitter; husband of Mara Sobieski.

Babysitters

Frank Cardova: long-time babysitter of Charlemagne; later, head of The Section; real name is Leo Vilseck; Section nickname is Buddy.

Justin Goodwin: FBI special agent and IT specialist; no aliases.

John Nakamura: official game name; real name unknown; usually called by his Section nickname, Skosh.

Jay Turner: FBI counterintelligence agent with a private agenda; no aliases.

Family members

Alexandra Sobieski: widow of Vasily Sobieski and daughter of former Charlemagne babysitter and head of Section Fred Dolnikov; no aliases. Now married to Mack.

Maryann and Theresa Vilseck: wife and daughter of Leo Vilseck, aka Frank Cardova.

Sally and Danny Kessler: ex-wife of and son of Steve Donovan.

GLOSSARY OF TERMS

AK-47 - developed by Mikhail Kalashnikov in 1947, one of the most ubiquitous firearms worldwide. It is reliable, uses standard 7.62 x 39mm ammunition, is inexpensive and fully automatic. Pretty much standard issue for insurgents and terrorists everywhere.

Babysitter - a government officer or agent responsible for the care, feeding, and security of a specialist under contract to that government, as well as for the fulfillment of the contract.

Beretta - an Italian-made weapon by the oldest continuous manufacturer of firearms in the world.

Dangle - slang for an otherwise uninvolved person used as bait in an operation to trap a target.

Glock - semi-automatic pistol manufactured by an Austrian company.

HK - Heckler & Koch, a German manufacturer of popular automatic weapons, especially submachine guns and assault rifles.

M-16 - 5.56 mm American military assault rifle.Running point - a term used in military and business applications to designate the lead in an operation. In a specialist operation, the position requires stealth and silence in removing especially dangerous obstacles such as watchers and snipers.

SAS - Special Air Service, the special forces unit of the British Army founded in 1941.

SCIF - Sensitive Compartmented Information Facility, a secure facility used by American and British military, security, and intelligence service to process sensitive compartmented information.

SIG Sauer - a German Swiss firearms manufacturer.

Specialist - an outside operative used by a government in extremely sensitive situations in which death of the opponent is likely and/or desired.

Tango - military slang for a hostile operative, usually a terrorist.

touch - a listening tap.